FAMILY ROYALE

AVERY BLAKE

STERLING & STONE

FAMILY ROYALE

Chapter One

DENNIS LOOKED around his shitty one-bedroom apartment, hating everything except the second chance sitting on the couch next to him — his sixteen-year-old son, Orin.

He didn't like the controller's odd weight, sleek and perfectly molded. The second he set it down, his hand felt like something was missing. A lot like how he felt holding a glass tumbler. Like addiction was kissing his skin.

And he didn't like the way the game looked. It was unsettling. The uncanny valley only existed in modern games because it was a bit creepy to control people that looked perfectly human. Things were simpler with the video games Dennis grew up with; you controlled a yellow circle eating ghosts, or more cartoonish versions of people. There was always some distance between the game and reality.

"Got ya!" Orin yelled, a look of pure joy on his face as he killed the opposing team's top player.

"Good job." The compliment felt unnatural, but Dennis needed something to get the conversation flowing.

Orin wasn't Dennis, and Dennis wasn't his father.

He didn't have to like the things his son liked, or even understand them. He had to love his son for whoever he wanted to be. Support that boy so he would turn into the kind of man a father like him could be proud of. And he would be, unlike his piece-of-shit dad.

Dennis was sired by an asshole, so he endeavored to do better, no matter what. And for a while, he did. Impressively, even. Susan was a veterinarian and Dennis was her assistant. They fell in love and had a kid, faster than most, but not as fast as some. Soon enough it made more sense for Dennis to stay home. The cost of daycare alone made the argument for them.

So he took their baby to playgroup twice a week, and to the park all the other days, at least once and twice more often than not. He cooked and cleaned, did all he could to keep Susan and Orin happy.

He was never much of a drinker, swearing away from the stuff, except for a few occasional drops, mostly to prove he was social. Alcohol had been the poison that consistently turned his father from Jekyll to Hyde. His father poured himself a glass to forget, a glass to remember, and a glass when nothing else happened to be going on, which according to his old man was most of the goddamned time.

Dennis could never relate, until the day he could, and found himself emptying a bottle before Susan got home. Orin was in kindergarten, and she didn't need him coming in, overstaffed as she was, requiring time away from all the overwhelm of an "always-on relationship," while still needing a warm body to get Orin to and from school, and tend things at home.

Unfortunately, she didn't need a warm body for much of anything else.

They started bickering back and forth. First a little,

then quickly a lot. Between that and the boredom, the bottle felt natural. More like a friend than temptation.

He kept drinking, finding the lies easier and easier to tell himself, naturally leaving his lips to burn the ears of anyone who would listen. Drank and drank until the bottles were drained, same as his life. What was black became blacker, both inside and out, until every day was another attempt to crack the walls of oblivion, and storm the fortress for himself.

Susan told him she never wanted to see him again, and she meant it.

Dennis had to hit bottom before declaring enough, then never again after that.

Now here was his second chance, and he wasn't going to blow it.

What difference did it make if Dennis lived in a dump he could barely afford, because all of his credits went to Susan. Every week of every month, all damned year long?

It didn't matter that they were sitting next to each other on a shitty secondhand sleeper couch, or that his juke had three owners before him. The game was new, the latest and greatest version of *HardCorps*, a multiplayer powerhouse that Dennis didn't even like when he was Orin's age.

The only thing that mattered was that their relationship had been strained for years, and now, just a month before his son turned sixteen, Dennis was finally going to fix it.

He accepted full responsibility. He drank too much, cared too little, and wasn't honest in the ways he should have been. Not with Susan, and not with himself.

But that didn't give her the right to ruin his life, both then and now, expect all his money, or sour the relationship he could have had with Orin these last few years while doing his best to rebuild himself. They could have moved on from all that old mess a while ago, but at least they were moving on from it.

It was water under the bridge. His son was here with him now, and Dennis was finally getting the chance to be a good father to Orin all over again.

He was different from the boy he'd been. Of course, he was almost sixteen. Dennis remembered what it'd been like with his own father at that age, and felt grateful that the cycle was broken. Proud of his determination, unwilling as he was to let history repeat itself, even knowing as he did that fathers and sons must sometimes struggle. How could they not, with one always working to maintain his power, while the other wished for independence?

Dennis had been thinking of something to say for a while, but the mood felt uncertain enough without him working to splinter it. He got hurt whenever Orin acted short or irritated with him, and in their few hours together so far, that had happened plenty already. It would be better to focus on the game, but the frame rate moved too fast, and was making him squeamish.

More than he wanted to admit.

Enough to make him feel like he wasn't the cool dad he wanted to be.

The game itself was disturbingly violent. The design itself was almost comedically over-the-top, as if that was supposed to make the savagery acceptable. Characters didn't die when you shot them, they exploded in what looked like a Fourth of July display of bloody guts and dripping nuggets of organ.

Orin laughed every time. Dennis laughed along with him, but he never meant it, and was sure his strained chuckles were obvious.

But Dennis didn't have to like the game, he just had to have fun playing it with Orin. And they weren't going to have fun until they were used to playing together. So for now, he swallowed his discomfort, kept his eyes on the TV screen split horizontally to show both players' POVs, and enjoyed *HardCorps* as the bonding agent with his son that he wanted, and maybe even needed, it to be.

Dennis's character took a sniper's bullet and turned him into a chunky puddle of crimson.

Another player — not the one who shot him — appeared out of nowhere, reached into the bloody pile and picked up what looked like his spinal cord. Then he used it to whip the broken pieces of Dennis's body, staining the green grass in a garish shade of red.

"Is that really necessary?" He tried to sound cool instead of disgusted.

"It's funny." Orin laughed.

Onscreen, a new character spawned.

Dennis didn't want to play anymore, but at least now they were talking. Sort of.

"So what are you doing in school? It's three hours of social per day, right?"

"Yep." Orin's gaze was fixed on the screen.

A beat, then, "What do you and your friends like to do?"

"Play *HardCorps*."

His tone was flat; Dennis was an idiot for asking. "Are you into any girls?"

Orin shrugged, the picture of indifference.

"How about college? Are you thinking about college? It's not like when I was a kid. You don't really even have to—"

"Shit, Dad!" Orin reeled around and gave Dennis a dirty look. "I can't concentrate with you constantly asking me questions. I just died, thanks a lot!"

Translation:

Stop interrogating me!

I just wanted to play this game Mom won't let me play, and I'm waiting for you shut the hell up and finally go to bed so I can log on and play with my friends.

Dennis was almost sixteen once himself. He understood, even if the situation was different. They would work this out, however long it took. He cared, unlike his own asshole father. And just like he had for so long, ever since he was a child, then before, during, and after the drinking, Dennis heard his dad's old words ringing in his ears.

I gave you everything, you little shit, you fucking pussy! And this is the thanks I get?

No, he certainly wasn't his father. But in the meantime, Dennis still had to draw a line.

He picked up the remote, turned off the TV, and turned to Orin. "Time for bed."

"*What?* It's only ten o'clock!"

"Right. That's bedtime."

"My bedtime is eleven."

"You mean when you're with your mother."

"Right. In the place where I live, and spend ninety-nine percent of my time."

"Not anymore. Weekends are mine. And you really expect me to believe that your mother lets you play this game? I doubt it, and I'm sure you don't want me to ask her. Am I wrong?"

Orin glared at him, then after a long moment said, "No."

"And I assume you want to play some more *HardCorps* tomorrow?"

"Of course, but that doesn't mean I want to get the third degree about every little thing."

"I'm not giving you the third degree, I'm trying to have a conversation."

Orin tucked a long lock of hair behind his ear and in a sulking voice that could only belong to a teenager said, "Well, it's really hard to talk and play at the same time."

"Exactly. That's why I turned it off."

Orin huffed, stood, then started marching toward the bathroom, mumbling under his breath. Dennis could only catch a few of the words, something about it being *worse here than with Mom*.

Not the best start to their first weekend together, but it wasn't a total disaster. They did have some fun, and Dennis kept reminding himself of the way his son had smiled when *HardCorps* was booting up, the first time he could see something almost pleasant on Orin's face, an expression that said a weekend with his father might not be so bad.

If he could find other ways to initiate that same expression, that didn't rely on realistic gore — no matter how exaggerated the graphics were supposed to be — then things would be headed in the right direction.

Dennis hated every minute of being a single dad to a teenage boy. But this was only the start, and things would get better. Like any kind of recovery, he would only get where he needed to go one step at a time.

Still, listening to Orin furiously brushing his teeth in the bathroom, Dennis couldn't help but remember the little boy he and Susan brought into this world. Before everything fell apart. The one who looked up into his eyes with admiration and wonder; the one who couldn't wait for their Scout meetings every Monday after dinner; the one who would rather be with him than not.

They used to be a team. Orin was learning to be a Scout, but Dennis was learning to be a father, ignoring the lifetime of lessons that warped him. He had the chance to start over with his own son. Do it right. And for a while, he did.

Even after Orin had started kindergarten, they used to go camping. Growing together, learning to tie knots, predicting the weather, and identifying constellations in the sky. Sure, they made mistakes, and their whittling never looked anything like it was supposed to, but it also never mattered. They would just laugh, grab another stick, and try again.

But thanks to some big mistakes, which Susan worked hard to balloon into something even bigger, all of that had been taken away from him. He'd made some mistakes, but Dennis wasn't his father. He and Orin were close, and back before his drinking, Dennis had been judgmental of parents who complained about the teenage years.

Of course it wasn't easy, and it required a lot of yourself, but wasn't that the point of being a good parent, to do the hard but necessary work of staying connected with their children? Dennis refused to let history repeat itself, and thus he was much closer with his son than most fathers. He understood how to communicate, to teach in a way that let his son understand what life was all about. His father's teaching style, by contrast, had been to throw Dennis into the deep end whenever possible. Literally.

Dad took him to a coworker's house and tossed him into the pool. Stood on the deck with his arms crossed, telling a six-year-old Dennis not to be a pussy when he got bubbles in his nose and was sure he might drown. His parents fought all the way home, Mom yelling at Dad.

That's no way to raise a child, Victor.

She was right, and it was the last thing Dennis ever wanted to be. Even now, after all those years where he'd been forced to stay away, Dennis was still a better father than the one who raised him. And this was his chance to prove it.

Orin emerged from the bathroom as Dennis finished

converting his crappy couch into an even crappier bed, trying to ignore a bitter wind coming in from a thin crack in the sliding glass door, that wouldn't quite seat itself in the threshold of his flimsy balcony.

He would improve that particular situation the second he could afford it. Get a brand new sofa bed. Or even better, move into a two-bedroom so his son could have some privacy.

"I made up the bed for you."

"Thanks," Orin said, sounding indifferent. "But I'm not ready."

Dennis didn't want to argue, but he had to stand his ground unless he was fine with Orin walking all over him.

"You can't play any more *HardCorps*."

"Got it."

"So what are you going to do?"

"I have homework," he said, pulling a tablet out of his backpack.

Dennis bit his tongue. Orin was obviously using school work as an excuse to stay up. He knew the trick well, used to pull it on his own father. It was one of the better ones, seeing as no reasonable parent would ever to tell their child to ignore their homework.

"Okay," Dennis said, feeling defeat but not wanting to let it show.

He went over to the kitchen without another word and began to load the dishwasher. His crap apartment had an open floorplan, probably because the builders couldn't afford too many walls, so the only thing separating him from his son was a shabby counter between them. Dennis was setting the first plate into the ancient machine when he heard the unmistakable chime of a messaging app. It sounded like the opposite of homework.

Orin scrambled to silence it, muting the app instead of

turning it off. Dennis wasn't dumb enough to be fooled, but he might be just smart enough to let it go.

Where would an argument possibly get him — especially on their first night together?

So he swallowed, loaded the second plate, and told himself to ignore it.

But Dennis wasn't sure he could. Because after a few minutes it became so blatant, it was as if Orin was waving a flag in front of his face. The app was muted, but his son's laughter was not. His fingers would blaze across the screen, followed by a pause as his friend, or friends, answered, then Orin would laugh and his fingers would start gliding across the glass yet again.

He really should say something.

But Dennis kept chewing on his tongue instead.

It was Friday night, and the first they were spending together. It would be a big mistake, starting things off with a fight. He could imagine Susan arriving on Sunday to find a scowling Orin, then glaring at Dennis with her smug, knowing expression.

See. It isn't as easy as you think it is, Dennis.

He had big plans for the weekend, starting tomorrow morning. But first they had to get through tonight. They were headed to the lake, where the fish would be as plentiful as the memories. Their day would be just like old times, or at least the right kind of echo. A reminder of what they once shared. So they could both find their best versions of themselves and finally reconnect.

Dennis looked across the counter. At least Orin looked happy. His smile was wide, and more genuine than anything he'd seen since Susan dropped him off a few hours ago. Did he expect that things would be magically back to the way they had been when Orin was a boy, just because Dennis wanted them to be?

He had to earn his way back, and that was fine. He'd never been afraid of working hard. He was up at five-thirty every weekday morning so he could be there to open the doors of Furry Friends at least five minutes to seven, and be there to receive all the precious pets from owners on their way to work. That was one of the only truly valuable things his father taught him. The old man had a hundred ways of saying the same thing, but they all made sense to Dennis.

You don't deserve *anything in life, son. You have to work for what you want.*

How badly you want something dictates how hard you're willing to work to get it.

You don't get what you want. Not ever. But most of the time, you get what you work for.

Dennis agreed, and was willing to do the work. Whatever it took to fix this.

But when he passed the couch on his way to the bedroom, and peeked over Orin's shoulder to see what he was typing, Dennis saw something that cleaved his heart into unfortunate halves.

my dad sux

And he thought: *What if my son really does hate me?*

Chapter Two

THE RENTED fishing boat reminded Dennis of how much Susan had taken from him.

Dennis used to have a small boat that he planned to love forever. Even gave it a silly name: *Wet Dream.* Susan never appreciated either the vessel or its moniker, and gave him plenty of shit about it. But Dennis always thought she was wrong about that, same as so many other things. The name was funny, not inappropriate.

What are you going to do when he asks what that means? Will you still think it's funny then?

Yes, of course he would. And Dennis told her so, every time she asked. He never understood what the big deal was. Why raise their son to be ashamed about the things that would eventually happen to his body? That was the worst way to raise a child. All the parenting books agreed on that, at least. So did Susan, until the truth made her uncomfortable.

Now Dennis had missed that part of his son's life. There was probably nothing he could teach his son about sex that Orin hadn't already heard from his friends, or seen for himself online.

Dennis would earn his spot back, and eventually Orin would feel comfortable talking to him. But for now they had to take it one conversation at a time, and their crappy rental didn't have any name whatsoever, humorous or otherwise.

Not that Dennis was foolish enough to believe that a fishing boat would cut down on his son's whining or sulking. Orin didn't want to be on the lake, nor did he want to be with his father, and he was doing everything in his power to subtly and not so subtly let him know it.

"When can we go home?"

"I told you, after we catch some fish."

"How about we stop at Provisions and buy ourselves some fish. Then we don't have to waste so much of our Saturday sucking."

Dennis chewed on the inside of his cheek, smiling as though he wasn't agitated in the least. "You know that's not the same. And besides, it's not about catching the fish so much as *catching the fish.*"

"Wow, Dad. That sounds *really* wise."

"I don't remember you being this much of a smartass," Dennis said before he could stop himself.

With the speed of a bullet, Orin replied, "Probably because drinking kills brain cells and negatively affects a person's memory."

Then he took out his phone, swiped a few times, and started laughing.

"Put that away," Dennis told him.

Orin didn't look up, or respond in any way.

"You've been on that thing nonstop. I need you to put it away, at least until we're done out here and back in the car, okay?"

Orin ignored every word from his father's mouth and said, "My friends are at the mall. Can you drop me off on the way home? Mom would be cool with it. She takes me all the time."

Dennis didn't know what to say. Everything felt like a battle, with him trapped on the losing end. It hadn't even been a day, and he was already exhausted.

This was special, and step one was getting Orin to understand that. Dennis spent an entire childhood dying to go fishing with his father, and yet was always left at home. It wasn't until Dennis was an adult when he finally realized that his old man never gave even the slightest of shits about fishing. A day in the boat was his way of getting the hell out of his house, retreating to place where he could drink the weekend away without getting nagged to death by his wife. But little Dennis had no idea, and spent all those Saturdays and Sundays with his mother believing he wasn't worthy, desperately waiting for his father to decide otherwise.

"Put it away," Dennis said. "And we'll talk about it on the way home."

"You mean talk about you dropping me off at the mall?"

"Sure."

Orin stowed the phone in his pocket, clearly irritated.

The silence was unsettling. Even the lake seemed desperate to scream.

Dennis finally cut into the quiet. "So how was your homework last night?"

And Orin snapped, "It's bad enough that you dragged me out here to go fishing — now you're going to interrogate me about my homework?"

"I'm not interrogating you," Dennis said, hurt.

Jesus, none of this is going according to plan.

15

"You used to love fishing."

"Yeah … when I was *ten*."

Dennis wanted to reach over, grab a handful of Orin's hair, and drag the unappreciative little shit down into the lake.

Instead he said, "You're being an ungrateful little asshole, you know that? Most kids don't have a dad who would take them fishing, or even want to spend time with them."

Orin looked almost thoughtful, and for a full moment, Dennis was naive enough to feel a wash of hope. But then his son delivered the punchline.

"Maybe you should adopt one of those kids. Then you'll have someone to kiss your ass for being such a great dad. Maybe they'll even get you a mug. It can say *World's Best Dad*, and you can fill it with whiskey."

That hurt. A lot. But Dennis couldn't let it show. Not on his face, or in his words. He had to swallow his ire. It wouldn't do any good to tell Orin what he was thinking, or share any of the painful memories that would probably only invite scorn or ridicule.

But they were there, as hurtful now as the day they happened.

Orin didn't have a clue, had no idea how lucky he was. Dennis was tempted to tell him, but now wasn't the time.

Still, he wished he could sever the memory, but no matter what he did it kept playing in a loop through his thoughts. Dennis couldn't stop thinking about the day he finally left for good, his father's words like poison on his lips.

I gave you everything, you little shit, you fucking pussy! And this is the thanks I get?

It cut as sharply now as it did on that awful afternoon

when he finally won his freedom, and an escape from his father's tyranny.

Dennis couldn't let history repeat itself.

He had to figure out a way to connect with his son.

This would all be so much easier if Susan hadn't poisoned Orin against him.

After another several minutes of deafening silence, Dennis finally told him to turn the boat around. The relief on Orin's face was yet another punch to the gut.

At least they had the ride back into town, and yet another chance to make everything better.

They made it back to the dock without a word passed between them.

Orin grabbed his backpack and got out of the boat, while Dennis secured the vessel and returned the fob to the office.

"Nothing biting, eh?" The man behind the desk was chewing on a Slim Jim, eyeing Dennis with a knowing smile. Maybe lots of fathers tried and failed to bond with their asshole sons on this lake.

"Not today," he answered with a weary smile.

Dennis stepped out of the rental office, looking left, right, and everywhere else, but seeing him nowhere. It took five full minutes to find him. Nowhere near the car, Orin was over in the picnic area, sitting on top of a table, texting on his phone.

Fine. They needed to eat anyway.

Dennis went to the car, grabbed the cooler, walked back over to the picnic benches, and plopped it down on the seat beside his son.

Orin didn't look up.

Dennis opened the cooler and divided their food into two piles. Peanut butter and jelly sandwiches, carrots and celery sticks, salt and vinegar potato chips, and soda. It was their old weekend special, including the grape-flavored carbonation he could barely tolerate, but that Orin had always loved.

They ate in silence, while Orin kept swiping on his phone, reading and laughing, acting like his father wasn't even there.

Maybe he'd been naive, thinking this would all naturally fall into place. Dennis wasn't sure what Susan had told him about everything, and their sour history might be a bigger problem than he was giving it credit for. It was probably time to address the elephant in the room.

"Put it away," Dennis told him again.

Orin looked up, but only barely. "Why?"

"Because I want to talk."

"This sounds like fun," he said, finishing whatever he was doing, before slipping the phone into his pocket. "What do you want?"

Dennis answered honestly. "Eventually, for you to be nice to me, but for now I'll settle for a conversation."

Orin rolled his eyes, and Dennis let it go.

"I don't know what you remember about the time before the divorce, or what your mother might've told you—"

"I remember you coming home falling-down drunk. Is that what you mean?"

Dennis swallowed. "Yes, that happened a few times."

"More than a few."

"Okay, that happened. But I've been sober for three years now."

"Yeah, good for you, Dad. You should wear the chip around your neck. That way everyone can see it and you won't have to announce it all the time."

A deep breath, then, "I don't 'announce it all the time.'

Unless I'm wrong, I think it's the first time I've told you that."

"I'm sure it won't be the last."

"I got sober for you, Orin. Because I wanted to be a better father for—"

"No way." Orin shook his head. "Don't put that on me."

"I'm not putting anything on you. I just want you to know that I'm trying. Help me do better. Tell me what you need so I can—"

"You want to know what I want?"

"Yes. Please."

"I want you to stop treating me like a kid. I'm practically an adult now."

Dennis wanted to loudly disagree. Hair on your balls didn't make you a man.

"Then talk to me. Maybe it's hard for me to stop seeing you as a kid because I don't know what's going on in your life. If we went to a restaurant you wouldn't expect the waitress to guess what you wanted, right? You would look at the menu, figure out what sounded good, then tell her so she could give it to you, right?"

"What if it was a waiter instead of a waitress?"

"Come on, Orin. Don't be a smartass. This can either work or not. I'm doing everything I can, so the rest is up to you."

Orin opened his mouth, upper lip curled into a smirk, but then he closed it. Appeared thoughtful for a moment, then managed to surprise the hell out of Dennis.

"There's this girl I like, but she's into Ryan."

"Ryan Wilder?"

Orin nodded, and Dennis thought, *Fuck the Wilders.*

He hadn't seriously thought about Thomas Wilder in years, but all the old hate came bubbling back up to the surface. Mister perfect, with his flawless life and his faultless son, always rubbing everything in Dennis's face. He was the kind of guy who only knew how to compliment others on the path to flattering himself.

"She's probably just into the car his daddy bought him," Dennis guessed, remembering that Ryan was a few months older than Orin, and that of course he would get a car on his sixteenth birthday.

Orin surprised him again, this time with the hint of a smile. "Yeah, it is. His dad got a new AUTOnomous X, but instead of trading in, he gave the old one to Ryan. How did you know?"

"Maybe I pay attention more than you give me credit for."

Orin bit into his sandwich, that smile growing.

And now Dennis was irritated. Same way he had always felt when hearing the name Thomas Wilder. He'd hated the guy for more than a decade. Wilder wasn't just everything Dennis wished he could be, he was a smug little asshole about it all. Highly successful — with the car, house, and family to prove it. Showboating while he volunteered. He and Ryan seemed close, and ever since kindergarten Dennis had been forced to hear all the other parents using him as a sterling example of what a father-son relationship should be like. The worst was hearing it from Susan.

At the talent show when Orin was ten, the Wilders did a duet that should have gotten them laughed off the stage. Tom played guitar and both of them sang. The whole thing was sappy and ridiculous, but the audience ate the absurdity like jelly in a donut, deciding to like it before the performance even started.

The opposite felt true for Dennis and his son. He had talked Orin into a performance of the classic "Rap God," by Eminem. They practiced all the words and worked tirelessly on their breath control. But they stumbled anyway, and were mercilessly heckled until they were forced to slink off-stage. Kids at school called Orin Rap Dog for the rest of the year.

"A car's not the only way to impress a girl, you know. How about we stop by the mall like you wanted, and get something cool to wear?"

"We can't do that by shopping at Dr. Discount."

"It doesn't have to be Dr. Discount. Where do you want to go?"

"You ever heard of Très Bien?"

"Of course I've heard of Très Bien."

Dennis had been out of debt for less than three months, and even now was living paycheck to meager paycheck. Très Bien was firmly out of a veterinary assistant's price range. They couldn't make a habit of it, but this was their first weekend together, and Dennis was determined to make it special however he possible could.

"So can we go?"

"Of course we can." Dennis smiled.

Orin actually smiled back, flicking a potato chip at his father, just like he used to.

And same as the old days, Dennis flicked one right back, fully unearthing a hope he'd been nursing for years.

Chapter Three

IT MAY NOT HAVE BEEN the best day of Dennis's life, but it was his best one in years.

They were back at the apartment. Dennis was sitting sprawled on his sleeper sofa, exhausted but happy. Things kept getting better and better after their awkward morning at the lake. Conversation in the car on the way back was engaging rather than labored. They didn't discuss anything deep, like he hoped they would, but there were signs that they would definitely get there.

Over the last few years of getting sober, Dennis had played all the important conversations over in his head.

He wanted to talk to Orin about saving money, because most kids were awful about that. Dennis turned eighteen, got more offers for credit than he could possibly refuse, then kept buying and buying because everything felt free, and ended up drowning in debt before he could legally drink.

But that wasn't a conversation to have on their way to shop at an overpriced store like Très Bien.

Dennis wanted to give his son warnings about FuckIt, and all the other online streaming services offering unlimited porn. It was a danger to the brain, and of course Dennis worried about Orin's developing mind. He wanted to warn him about the ups and downs of depression, and how too much porn could feed the wrong things in the wrong ways. And, perhaps most importantly, he wanted to warn his son about the disease that had poisoned their bloodline, and that even a few drops of the stuff might be too much.

But that could all come later.

Today had been about fun, exactly as it should have been. Shopping, pizza, and ice cream. Dennis finally had his son back. Sure, he had blown through almost a hundred credits, or the equivalent of nearly three days' pay. But he wasn't thinking about that.

Instead Dennis kept picturing Orin's giant smile while trying on his new shoes, looking at his reflection, and primping in that brand new jacket.

There was no reason to think about the day's tab when Orin was opening up to him, telling his father stories about the social blocks at school. Who said what to whom. He didn't get super personal there, but he would in time. For now it was just two guys shooting the shit, and that made it easy for Dennis to feel like his son finally trusted him again.

"Tell me more about this girl you're into. The one who likes Ryan."

Orin shrugged, leaning forward to grab his grape soda from the coffee table. "There isn't much to tell."

"What does she look like?"

"She's taller than most of the girls. About an inch taller than me. But I like that." He laughed. "I think she's hot."

"They still have dances and social stuff like that, right?"

"That's pretty much all it is now. We're supposed to get all our work done at home, or online. School is for the teachers to check on us, and so we can socialize."

"When is the next dance?"

"I don't know. I never go."

"Aren't you supposed to go?"

"They're not mandatory, and mom never makes me."

"What's the girl's name?"

"Phoebe."

"So why not go and ask Phoebe?"

"Because she's probably going with Ryan."

"But you don't know that, do you?"

Orin considered, then after a quiet moment shook his head.

"Well," Dennis said, "If you don't ask her, then what other choice does she have? Sounds to me like you might be throwing Phoebe right into his arms."

Orin actually looked like he was processing his father's words. It'd been years since Dennis had felt so encouraged.

The silence wasn't awkward like before. Now it was pleasant, almost a shame to break it. But his heart was beating harder, encouraging Dennis to speak his mind.

"You know, it's been six years since the divorce."

"That's the one after five, but right before seven, right?" But Orin was laughing, including his father in the joke instead of making him the butt of it.

"Right," Dennis laughed back. "Your mom has had custody that entire time. And for good reasons. But maybe it's time to switch things up. You're going to be sixteen soon, and you do have a voice here. If you told the court that you wanted to live with me, I'm sure they would listen. And then your mother would have to."

Orin looked around his father's crap pad, then kindly

he said, "I'm not sure there's enough space here for both of us. It's fine for a weekend, but …"

He let it hang, because the rest was obvious.

"Oh, of course. I would move. You're almost a man, you deserve your own room. Everyone needs their own space, but especially teenage boys. Remember, I used to be one myself."

"Yeah, I was just about to forget that." Another laugh warmed Dennis even more than the last one. "No offense, but if you can move, then why do you live here?"

"Because most of my credits go to your mom for child support. But that wouldn't be the case if you were living with me. Right now I'm paying both alimony *and* child support. If I had all of that money each month, we could live wherever you wanted."

Orin obviously didn't hate the idea. He seemed to be thinking, and that's all Dennis wanted. It was already more than he expected to get their first weekend together, especially considering the way things had been between them just twenty-four hours ago.

"If Mom decides to marry Rick, then I'd definitely want to live with you."

A lovely surprise. He knew that Susan and Rick were considering tying the knot, but not that Orin might have a problem with it.

"You don't like Rick?"

Orin shrugged, and Dennis studied his gesture. It seemed to him like maybe he didn't care for his mother's boyfriend all that much, but didn't necessarily want to discuss it.

Still, Dennis was tempted to dig for details. If Rick was a bad influence on his son, then that was another argument he could use in his custody battle. The judge would want to know that, and Dennis would have no problem telling him.

He was thinking about the best way to word his next question when Orin's phone buzzed on the coffee table.

He picked it up, looked at the screen, then turned to his father. "My friends want to play *HardCorps*. You mind if I log on?"

"Of course not. Mind if I play, too?"

Orin hesitated, a moment too long, and Dennis wondered if it was a mistake to ask.

But the day continued to surprise him.

"Sure," Orin said.

They logged on, and Dennis tried to keep up, immediately realizing that he was playing a very different game from the one last night. Orin had obviously been going easy on him, dicking around, waiting for his dad to get bored and turn the thing off so he could play with his friends.

Orin was good, and maybe even great. He must be a natural, or play a lot with his friends, because he always knew where to hide, and never seemed to miss a shot.

"Great shot, Mr. Hoke!" said one of Orin's friends, even though it wasn't.

"That always happens to me," said another, though Dennis didn't even know what had happened.

"You'll do better next time!" They continued to encourage him, though he couldn't help but feel like they were all laughing at him, and waiting for him to go away.

"Are there any missions, or is it all just battle royale?"

Orin looked over at his father. "You want to go on a mission?"

"I don't know." Dennis shrugged. "Are they any fun?"

He turned back to the game without offering his father an

answer, but after that round finished he pressed some buttons, cycling through several screens, until it paused on a picture showing all seven members of their team, including Dennis, whose character looked like some sort of angry Mad Hatter.

The screen said, *Get your prisoner to the landing strip!*

Dennis didn't know exactly what that meant, but he was glad to have an objective.

Unfortunately, he stepped on a landmine, and killed their collective game less than sixty seconds after it started. Orin looked deeply disappointed, and Dennis could feel the shame wafting off of his body.

"Well, that's it for me. I have to check in with the clinic, anyway."

He didn't.

Dennis set down his controller and stood from the sofa, trying to ignore Orin's obvious relief. "Have fun playing with the guys."

Halfway to the bedroom he heard Orin mumble into his headset, "I know, right?"

Maybe it was an apology to the team, or Orin thanking the guys for putting up with his dad's desire to play. Either way, Dennis felt more hurt than he cared to admit.

But still, at least he'd let him try.

There had been plenty of great things about the day to focus on. A perfect relationship wouldn't magically fall into place overnight. Rebuilding with his son was a long-term project. And while Dennis couldn't afford more days like this one, he shouldn't need to.

He wasn't out to buy his son's affection. Maybe that worked for Thomas Wilder, but Dennis probably didn't make even a tenth of the credits.

The thought hit him with a wave of bitterness. And since he didn't have anything to check on, Dennis figured he could use the time to see what his nemesis had been up to.

He logged onto LiveLyfe, and clicked over to Tom's profile. They were still friends on the platform, and while he'd done this before — many, many times — it had been a while. Back when Orin was in kindergarten, Dennis couldn't help himself. It was a sickness for sure.

But still so much better than his other one.

Dennis scrolled through Wilder's timeline, growing more agitated by the post. Hundreds of photos with him and Ryan, living the perfect life of a bonded father and son. According to his most recent post, they just got home from some high-tech military-style bootcamp where they were learning to shoot real weapons from retired Navy Seals.

And Dennis could barely stomach playing his son's video game.

He kept scrolling, past the pictures of a martial arts tournament. Ryan was competing, but Tom was bragging about his newest medal. *I'm so proud of him!*

Apparently Tom had to tell the world about every little accomplishment.

Share every stupid photo.

The next set showed them at some five-star restaurant in London, where he'd taken Ryan on a business trip so he could "learn the ropes" of running the company his son would someday inherit. The plates were big but the portions tiny. Entrees looked like appetizers, and a total waste of credits.

It was so unfair. Everything was easy for guys like Thomas Wilder. He was handsome and smart, so high school was probably a breeze. A good example of the rich getting richer. His parents could afford to send him to the very best schools, while Dennis had been lucky to learn a trade at a technical college that left him with bites and scratches on the best of days, in a job where he was over-worked, underpaid, and under-appreciated. Where being the low man on the totem pole meant he had been in charge of euthanizing the ailing animals, and "giving owners the gift of compassion, to alleviate their suffering" for over a year now.

As Dennis scrolled Wilder's old posts, a new one popped up, bragging about joining some ultimate chal-lenge called Millennial Knight, sponsored by famili, the new parenting app that the world couldn't seem to shut up about.

The famili app made a bold promise that was hard to believe, despite the results being hard to argue with. By pairing parenting with gamification, famili encouraged healthy habits through learned behaviors over rote instruction.

The concept itself was simple. Dogs were rewarded during their training. When they behaved well, they were given a treat. Dennis saw it at Furry Friends all the time, from the best-trained among the pets coming into the clinic.

The same was true with gamification. Complete a level, get a reward to reinforce the desired habit or behav-ior. It gave users a sense of accomplishment, which was one of the most powerful psychological driving factors for human achievement.

Everything a person did was done only to achieve something else, no matter how big or small that victory might be. Managing money, getting fit, or becoming a much better parent.

And now here was Wilder, singing famili's praises, telling the world how it had helped him smooth out some of the areas where he wasn't as good of a father, making Dennis want to find something to put his fist through.

He'd heard about famili plenty, but until Wilder's post he hadn't really given it a second thought. Now, reading all about the app, Dennis had to admit that it sounded like a fantastic idea. It combined real-life activities with virtual ones. Sort of like a reality show where anyone could enter. Users could earn points from the app's various challenges and audience attention. Smileys, shares, and comments, alongside player achievements. There was even a leader-board for the best parents, divided by region, age, ethnicity, or any other variable a user wanted to plug into the formula to see where they fared.

The media *loved* famili. Dennis couldn't remember another app ever getting so much positive attention. He supposed it made sense. Terrible parenting was probably the number one thing wrong with the world. But it also struck him as a little sad that a core duty like *being a good father* had to be turned into a game. And one Wilder was apparently great at playing, in addition to all the other things he was perfect at.

There were cash and prizes for the best parents — a ridiculously absurd sentence now that Dennis considered it. Everything from cash to cars, amazing vacations and cutting-edge gear, with new winners announced daily, weekly, monthly, and annually, depending on the particular contest or game. Flashing on the famili home screen now was an all-inclusive week at The Majestic, some ostentatious resort in the Grand Canyon where celebrities apparently loved to vacation away from the rabble.

Activities ran the gamut. Teaching your children about money management, doing chores, building simple things together. There were even some over-the-top challenges, not unlike some of the reality and game shows that Dennis and Susan used to stream on their juke.

Wilder's posts made him itchy with anger. That asshole didn't need the money; Tom could do all of that stuff with his kid. But his ego was so big, he just had to be #1 with absolutely everything.

Dennis hoped that some other father-son team signed up to kick his stupid ass.

Then it hit him. An epiphany from nowhere, and something that could change his life.

Improve his relationship with Orin for good.

What if they signed up for the famili app together?

Orin would love this. Some of the bigger games — like the Millennial Knight Tournament — reminded Dennis of *HardCorps*, after all. So he downloaded the app and began to explore it.

The design was remarkable. Using famili was intuitive and delightful. One of those apps he knew how to use the moment he started. He scrolled through his choices, selected *Father and Son*, then signed himself up for an account, along with Orin.

He did a search, found the Millennial Knight Tournament, and went to enter himself.

The fee was steep. Dennis couldn't afford it, even if he hadn't spent a hundred credits to pay for his very memorable afternoon. But with all of the cash and prizes, including a grand prize of 10,000 credits, coupled with a fierce determination to win, and Orin's skills as a Scout, his risk of not recovering the admittedly ample sum was greatly reduced.

Dennis could dust off his old manuals, give himself a refresher, then get ready to kick some serious father-and-son ass. Maybe they could win enough to pay off today's charges, while also having some unforgettable adventures.

This was a new opportunity to earn Orin's respect, maybe demonstrate to the courts that he deserved joint custody, at least.

Maybe the gamification was good.

Dennis was desperate for a win. A victory here would give him what he'd been longing for.

And what Orin probably needed most.

Chapter Four

THE NEXT MORNING, Dennis made pancakes.

And not just any pancakes. This was the same recipe Orin had loved as a boy. He used to beg his father to make them. No exaggeration. Once, when he was four or five, Orin cried for over an hour after Dennis told him he'd have to wait until the following Sunday. They ran out of flour, and he was too exhausted to make a grocery run. But the next weekend, he made four times as many pancakes — twice the amount each day, both Saturday and Sunday.

The batter was easier to make than it should have been, considering how light and fluffy the pancakes were. A little sweet, but not so much that Orin couldn't also drown them in syrup. The recipe even impressed Susan. She was amazed that his batches never had even a single sacrificial pancake. She always lost the first one. Either burned to a crisp, or white and raw in the middle.

Dennis wasn't a good cook, but he could make the hell out of his pancakes, and at least this morning that would be enough.

Orin gave his father an appreciative smile from behind

his overstuffed mouth. "Wow. These are as good as I remember."

"I'm glad you still like them. It's been years since I—"

"Don't stop." Orin shoved another fat forkful into his mouth.

"I'll make them the next time you come over?"

"Pee-doh." *Please do.*

"So, I have an idea."

Orin looked up. "Yeah?"

"Have you heard of famili?"

"Of course." *Duh.*

"I signed us up."

Orin obviously wanted to roll his eyes, but instead he said, "Why?"

"I thought it would be fun. I didn't just get us accounts with the app, I signed us up for one of the upcoming games."

He frowned. "That sounds like a lot of work."

"It's not work if it's fun, right? Aren't any of your friends doing it?"

"Um … no." *Because that would be lame, just like you.*

"Ryan is doing it with his dad. I saw it on LiveLyfe last night. They're signed up for the Millennial Knight Tournament. Same as us."

"Oh?" That got Orin's attention.

"I thought it might be fun for you to beat him at something. Maybe, you know …" Dennis gave him a knowing smile, hoping he would get it. "Impress a certain someone."

"Millennial Knight, huh? That's the big one."

"You've heard of it?"

Orin shrugged. "I get the ads all the time, and that one has the best prizes from what I've seen. How long do we have to get ready?"

"A little over three months."

"And you already signed me up?" Orin appeared slightly bothered. "Without even asking me if I wanted to do it?"

"Well, sure, but only because I was already signing myself up. You can always cancel."

"But you can't do it without me, because it has to be a child and their parent, right?"

"Well, yeah," Dennis admitted.

Orin didn't say anything else while he polished off his pancakes, but once the plate was empty except for a few scattered puddles of syrup still sticking to the melamine, he finally nodded. "Okay, let's do this thing. We're supposed to pick out our training activities, right? That's how this works? Please tell me you didn't do that for me already, too."

Dennis felt chastised, but told himself to ignore it. "No, of course not. Just the account."

"Cool."

And it was. Moments later they were looking at famili, scrolling through the options, searching for an activity they could do together. Something that would be fun, while also helping them to prepare for the tournament in another three months.

But already they weren't seeing eye to eye. Orin preferred the geekier challenges, that weren't as likely to help them. He wanted to play augmented reality games, or build robots for a miniature Bot Royale among some of the other hopefuls. When Dennis objected to both those ideas, Orin suggested an escape room. That might have sounded fine, if success wasn't reliant on knowledge of comic book and video game trivia that Dennis knew nothing about.

"Don't you think we should stick to the kind of challenges that'll help us win?"

"We have plenty of time for that," Orin said. "Don't you want to have fun?"

Of course he did. But Dennis was also practical, and the experience only came with so many training vouchers. He also understood what Orin obviously didn't. Practice made perfect, and the best time to start was before now. They would never beat the Wilders if they spent all their time opting into silly games over serious challenges.

"How about this one?"

Dennis pointed to a hiking trail, filled with obstacles and a capture-the-flag challenge at the end. Similar to what they would probably be facing in another few months. The tournament was part race, part battle in the wilderness, that ended with the capture-the-flag portion. They had experience as Scouts, and that gave them an advantage, but only if they were willing to use it.

Orin looked like Dennis had offered him a barrel full of vegetables.

Maybe he was right. If their first challenge was fun, they could do more later. But if they started with something he didn't really want to do, the whole thing might end up a battle.

"Why don't you choose the first one? Something fun for before your mother picks you up."

Without hesitation, Orin pointed to a team-based shooter that reminded Dennis of *HardCorps*, the live version.

"Okay!" he agreed, with all the enthusiasm he could muster.

Dennis rinsed their dishes and loaded them into the dishwasher. Then they left the apartment and climbed into his old car.

"We're going to BlastZone," he told the car, then it

pulled away from the curb and started driving them to the nearest virtual gaming center.

The cost per mission was more than Dennis expected, but he tried not to show the disappointment on his face as he held his phone over the terminal to pay. BlastZone wasn't one of the training challenges that came with a voucher. The place was independently run, and thus additional credits.

Dennis didn't like the pizza-faced teenager eyeing him as he handed over their VR headsets and suits, then issued their guns. But Dennis ignored that, too.

Their mission was straightforward, and again, not unlike what Orin was used to after an adolescence of secretly playing *HardCorps* and similar games with his friends. They were supposed to clear a terrorist-infested maze, and save the hostage waiting in a guarded room at the other end.

The basic layouts and enemies were the same, regardless of the skins participants chose. But since Orin was into sci-fi, their maze was in a space station, and the terrorists were all aliens.

Dennis also let him pick the potential prize. It didn't matter to him. They weren't here to win, he just wanted to have fun with his son, get comfortable with the idea of competing, familiarize themselves with the app.

Orin chose a free *ALL YOU CAN EAT!* dinner at El Burro, a fancy Mexican restaurant that all his friends apparently liked. Dennis had never been.

The game was hard, and he felt immediately out of his element. His only goal was to stay alive, and not embarrass himself or his son. But there were enemies everywhere, and Dennis kept getting shot.

"Stay down," Orin ordered.

And so he did.

"See that guy up in the tower …?" Orin pointed. "*Shoot him!*"

So Dennis shot him on his third try.

"Cover me, I'm heading for the entryway over there!"

It was simple enough to stay alive, once Dennis stopped trying to do everything his way, and relaxed into letting Orin lead the charge. He understood the space in a way that his father did not, and once Dennis started following orders, they began kicking heaps of ass together.

The more they kicked, the happier Orin became.

And the happier his son, the more Dennis wanted to please him.

They kept doing better and better, but he was still shocked when they finished the game in first place. Dennis had even nabbed a handful of bullseyes. And that was almost as great as his son's obvious pride.

"Looks like we're eating dinner at El Burro!" Orin said, beaming.

It might have been the happiest Dennis had felt in years, seeing Orin's glee, and knowing he'd nearly lost track of time while playing with his father.

Just like the old days.

One of the best parts of their afternoon, and something Dennis hadn't expected, was the audience online. Dennis wasn't used to being watched, and was surprised by the followers. One of them especially.

There were plenty of kind comments and congratulations, but right there at the top was one from Phoebe. Apparently it was easy to find them, since Orin had linked his famili and LiveLyfe apps together.

Nice to see you here, Orin! I'm rooting for you.

"Is that *the* Phoebe?" Dennis asked, even though he didn't need to when Orin's face told him the story.

"Yeah." His son was actually blushing.

"Take that, Ryan!"

Orin laughed. "Yeah, take that."

It was great to see him coming out of his shell. Dennis still thought it was weird, getting points for spending time with his son, even though he hadn't done any sort of mentoring during the game, or really any parenting at all. He'd followed Orin's directions, no differently than if he'd been holding a controller at home.

It felt a bit disingenuous, since as Dennis understood it, the point of the famili app was to become more involved. A better parent.

At least they were spending time together. That's where everything started. And it did feel gratifying to see their score. As long as they kept the famili app running in the background, their time at BlastZone was linked to their overall performance. They scored high enough to land them in the top twenty for the overall event, with totals from contestants pouring in from associated BlastZones and independent virtual gaming centers across the country.

Their gameplay had been recorded, with the footage of their avatars waiting in a dashboard to be replayed whenever they wanted. Even if Orin didn't want to watch it again, Dennis definitely did.

"Looks like you were right," he told Orin while sitting across from him at El Burro.

Susan would probably yell at him for ruining his dinner, but so what. They worked hard for the meal, and it had been years since he'd taken his son to a restaurant.

"About what?" Orin looked up from his menu.

"About which event to choose. You killed it."

"*We* killed it," Orin corrected.

"Sure, but only thanks to you. No way we would have

made the leaderboard our first time out, if we'd gone on the hiking trail like I wanted."

"True," he laughed, "that was a pretty crappy idea."

Dennis laughed back, because that time Orin was clearly kidding.

He put down his menu. "I have no idea what to order."

Dennis grinned, and leaned forward. "How about *whatever you want*? Our winning means it's all you can eat."

"I forgot about that!"

They didn't order everything, because they weren't allowed to-go boxes, and Dennis reminded his son that it wasn't good to be wasteful. But they got plates of enchiladas, a full order of nachos, two chile rellenos, five tacos to split between them, a massive bowl of table-side guacamole, and two kinds of dessert — sopapillas and deep-fried ice cream.

"So should we cash out our points?" Orin asked while they waited for their check.

"Why would we do that?"

"Because if we cash out, we'll get ten credits that can be used in the JukeStore."

"Right, but why not wait? Have you seen some of the bigger prizes?"

"Yeah," Orin said. "But we'll never get there. If we cash in now, I could buy more levels and skins in *HardCorps*."

Apparently, Orin didn't want to know if they should cash in their points, he wanted Dennis to tell him that was a good idea.

But it wasn't.

"If you wait, I bet we could earn enough points to eventually get a new juke altogether."

Orin's eyes went wide. Practically dilated. Dennis's juke was embarrassing. At least two generations old. It didn't bother him since he only used it for music and movies. But it apparently sucked for gaming, at least compared to the jukes all his friends were playing on. He'd heard Orin mumbling under his breath while he was booting it up on Friday night.

"Just give it some thought," Dennis suggested. "No pressure."

"No, you're right. We should save the points."

"Awesome."

"Yeah," Orin agreed. "Awesome."

Then he gave his father a smile that Dennis would be thinking about as he fell asleep, and would probably still think about when he woke in the morning.

The check came and Orin did the honors, holding his phone over the bill so their winnings could cover the total. Then they got in the car, chatting and laughing while it drove them home.

Susan was waiting when they arrived. Scowling at first, but then she must've seen the look on Orin's face. She immediately softened.

"Looks like you two had a good time."

"It was great," Orin said.

And Dennis felt even warmer.

HE COULDN'T SLEEP, partly because his stomach had half of Tijuana inside it, and the rest because he had too much going on in his head. Dennis was editing clips from the game, putting together a highlight reel he could watch over and over if he wanted to. But for now, he posted the clip to their famili page with the caption, *Dorky dad and his awesome son. Can't believe how well we did!*

It was fun to make, so Dennis posted another, then another. By the time he finished editing the fourth and final clip, reminding himself that he had work in the morning and really should get to bed, there were already a few enthusiastic comments on the first one.

Dennis was also surprised to realize that the game was giving additional points for positive comments, smileys, and shares. They could really beef up their score if he and Orin took the time to arrange a few more photogenic moments.

He scrolled through the commenters, stopping at a MILFy-looking avatar with the username @hawtestmom. She posted, *I really like the way you shoot that thing!*

Was she flirting with him?

Dennis definitely thought so. And he had to admit, it felt nice. He posted back: *I make sure it never goes off by accident.* And then, a winky-face.

The day had been full of victories, and Dennis should've left it at that. But he couldn't help himself, tapping over to check out how Team Wilder was doing before he even realized it.

Suddenly, the twenty-one followers he earned with Orin felt like nothing.

Because Tom and his son had over twenty-one *thousand*.

And all Dennis could think was, *How will we ever catch up?*

Chapter Five

It was the longest week of his life.

Dennis couldn't wait until Friday. He felt like such a dork, watching their videos from last Sunday each night before bed. But it made him so happy, watching the way Orin owned the space, seeing enemies almost as if he had X-Ray vision.

Where had he learned to shoot like that? There was no way Susan was letting him play *HardCorps* at home. How much sneaking around was he doing? Or was he really just that good?

All week long he made imaginary plans, picturing all the things he and Orin would do together after his mother dropped him off.

She was prompt like always, but her scrunched face reminded him of every argument they'd ever had.

"We need to talk," Susan said, confirming his fears, as Orin hugged him hello.

"Can you walk me out to my car?"

Super.

Obviously, she wanted to pick a fight about something.

That was always her thing, never argue in front of Orin, no matter what. The rule had led to a lot of closed-door conversations during that last year before the divorce. More than Dennis could count. Or, as Susan would probably say, more than he could remember.

They used to fight in front of Orin all the time, after Dennis started drinking, but before their marriage crumbled to nothing. According to Susan, it scarred Orin enough that it was a prime condition on Dennis getting him on the weekends. He wouldn't be surprised if that was Susan's rule more than Orin's.

"You took him to Très Bien?" Susan said more than asked, once they were standing in front of her car.

"Well, yeah. So?" Dennis already knew where this was going.

"Do you want to tell me why you did that?"

"No, but I'm guessing I'm supposed to." He laughed.

Susan didn't join him, staring back at her ex instead.

"It was our first weekend together in a long time. I thought it would be fun."

"Fun? That's not really the word I'd use. Indulgent, maybe. You could also go with permissive. Going to Blast-Zone, which I'm sure also cost a pretty penny, *that* sounds like fun. But Très Bien, really? What were you thinking?"

"Why does that bother you so much? I got him a jacket and a pair of shoes. Sorry if it made you look bad."

"Fuck you, Dennis. That's not what I care about."

Great, they were already swearing. Good to know.

"Then what *is it* that you care about, Susan? Why don't you tell me what it is I've done so wrong."

"I'm disappointed that you have to ask, or that we're even having this conversation."

"I'm sorry to be disappointing you yet again. Fortunately, you should be used to it by now."

"It's setting a bad precedent, and you know that. Neither of us can afford to buy things like that for our son on a regular basis."

"And?" Dennis wanted her to get on with it. He and Orin had some *HardCorps* to play.

"I'm worried about you."

"I doubt that. I'm sure you're worried about how I might be affecting you, or Orin, or your happy little family with Rick. But it's been a long damned time since you gave a shit about me."

"That's not true."

"We both know it is."

"Are you still going to your meetings every week?"

"Why would you ask me that?"

"Because, this is what you do. Overspending on gifts go with your drinking binges. And some of what Orin shared with me this week has me wondering if maybe you're hitting the bottle again."

"I haven't touched a drink in three years!" Then, because Susan got under his skin like no one else in the world, he added, "It's a lot easier now that I'm not living with you."

"I'm not trying to be a bitch here, Dennis. I'm asking a legitimate question. Because I'm worried about our son. And yes, believe it or not, I'm worried about you. I don't want to be married to you, but that doesn't mean I don't care about you. Or that I don't have feelings. You put us through hell with your drinking before, and Leanne told me that I need to be honest with you, or I can't expect a different result. So that's what this is, me being honest."

"Leanne, your shrink?"

"Yes, Dennis. Leanne, my *therapist.*"

"Please tell her I said thank you. I forgot how much I've missed this."

Susan stood straighter, firming her jaw. "At the first sign of your drinking, Orin will stop coming over. And if you don't like that, then you can pay for a lawyer to fight it. You got that?"

"For years now," Dennis said, working not to explode.

Of course he got it. He never had a choice. Susan had sole custody, and the court wouldn't even grant visitation after the judge discovered some of what he'd done. Orin was only with him now because Susan allowed it. She had all the power, and Dennis couldn't afford to forget it.

"Are you going to your meetings or not?"

"Yes," Dennis said, softer than before. "I swear. I go most nights after work. I'm happy to give you my sponsor's number if you feel like you need to check up on me."

"Thanks, but that won't be necessary."

"Glad to hear it."

"But I would still like to know why you spent so much on Orin. The shoes and that hoodie ... that had to run you at least fifty credits."

Try seventy-five.

"I won't always be able to afford it, I know that. But it's been a long time, and I guess I just wanted to show Orin how much I love him; how much I've missed him."

"You can't buy love, Dennis."

"That's The Beatles, right?" He wasn't trying to be a jerk, not really. He just didn't know what else to say. Everything out of Susan's mouth sounded like a criticism, and it was either this or fighting.

Susan sighed.

Dennis said, "Is there anything else you want to talk about? Orin and I have plans for tonight, and it would be nice to get started."

"He said something about some contest ... do you want to tell me what that's all about?"

"No, but I can if I have to."

Susan kept staring.

Dennis continued. "It's a father-son thing. Just some fun activities for us to do on weekends. To make our time more meaningful."

Susan looked skeptical, because of course she did. "I'm not sure that's a great idea—"

"Shocking."

"—considering how competitive you get."

"I don't get competitive."

She laughed. "Do you not remember T-ball?"

"I'm not going to push him. This is just for fun."

Susan opened her car door. "Make sure he's not late for school on Monday morning. He already has two tardies, and a third means detention."

"Got it. Thanks for trusting me with another night."

Her door closed and he added, "Have fun with Rick. Do that thing with your finger. He'll probably like it."

And then she drove away.

Chapter Six

DENNIS WASN'T ABOUT to let Susan get in the way of another awesome weekend with Orin, even if she had annoyed the shit out of him. He'd planned an awesome Friday night, starting with a meal they could cook together.

He bought everything at the grocery store that they would need to make a chili con carne fajita dish. Orin wanted to order it at El Burro, but they'd already asked for more than the two of them could polish off, even at their most gluttonous.

He liked things spicy. More than Dennis, and probably more than most kids his age, so he also bought lots of hot pepper sauce and fresh jalapeños to chop up and mix into the dish — two ingredients he would never have on his own.

Dennis was doing his best, but he could still feel Orin getting annoyed with him, especially when he insisted on taking pictures of "every little thing."

He shouldn't have to explain. Orin should understand this better than Dennis.

That was how the famili app worked. It's how life worked these days.

The more they documented their lives, the more they would be seen.

The more they were seen, the more chances they would have to be recognized.

The more they were recognized, the better their odds at gathering fans and the attention needed to go from good to great, and then from great into winners of the whole damned thing.

"Do you have to take pictures of *everything*?" Orin asked.

"No, not everything," Dennis said, taking a selfie of them standing together, behind the finished dish, in their matching aprons. "But the more pictures we take, the more we'll have to choose from. Don't worry, I'll do all the work. I just need you to smile."

He did, but Orin still looked embarrassed more than excited, so Dennis would have to figure out a way to fix that. They weren't going to win if that was a regular thing.

"You do want a new juke, right?"

"I think we established that, Dad."

"Well, social proof is a part of the game. A big part, so if we want to win, we'll have to take pictures."

"Do they have to be in aprons that say, *I'm 'bout to slap meat on your grill?* It's not even funny."

"These were the only aprons they had, other than the plain white ones."

"What was wrong with those … and why did we need aprons at all? Mom cooks every day, and I've never seen her in an apron."

"Yeah, your mom doesn't really like to dress up for things."

"What does that mean?"

"Nothing. One more, then we'll eat, okay?"

Orin begrudgingly complied, gritting his teeth through another photo, before inhaling his dinner.

"Slow down," Dennis suggested, careful to keep it from sounding like an order.

"I'm hungry."

"You can't be that hungry." Dennis grinned, still keeping it friendly. "Are you sure it isn't just that you want to log on and play *HardCorps* with your friends?"

Orin cracked a smile. "Maybe."

"Well then, let's make sure you have all the time you need to play. I definitely don't want to take that away from you. But I've been waiting all week for this. So let's have a nice dinner, then the juke is all yours. Deal?"

Orin immediately slowed the forkful of fajitas already on the way to his mouth, nodding. "Sorry, Dad."

"Tell me about your week."

He shrugged. "There's not much to tell."

"Did you ask Phoebe to the dance?"

Orin rolled his eyes. "No."

"Are you going to?"

"I don't know. Probably not."

"Why? She obviously likes you."

Orin looked at his father like he was crazy. "How can you possibly know that?"

"Nice to see you here, Orin!" Dennis did his admittedly awful impression of a teenage girl, in a high-pitched voice with a trill at the end. "I'm rooting for you."

"That doesn't mean anything. Everyone says stuff like that."

"I doubt *everyone* does."

"Pretty much."

"Okay," Dennis said, now changing the subject. "Why don't we make our weekend plans?"

"Sure." Orin perked up, but still wasn't nearly as excited as Dennis wanted him to be. "What do you want to do?"

"Whatever you do, so long as we're pulling ahead of Team Wilder. We want Ryan embarrassed enough to make Phoebe come running into your arms."

"Dad …"

"What?"

"Nothing," Orin shook his head. "I just wish I'd never told you."

"About Phoebe?"

"Yeah, about Phoebe."

"Why?"

"Because now you won't shut up about it."

Ouch.

"I'm not trying to be annoying, Orin. I'm on your side."

"Just pick something. I'm fine with whatever." Then he filled his mouth with fajitas.

"BlastZone was a great idea. Why don't you pick whatever sounds like the most fun to you. After dinner. Then you can play *HardCorps* with your friends for the rest of the night. Deal?"

Nodding, smiling, and chewing, Orin said, "Deal."

Dennis would never have picked either of Orin's selections, but both sounded like they might be a lot of fun if he was willing to open his mind. And, of course, he absolutely was, determined to make this weekend with his son even better than the last one.

His first selection was a ghoulish-sounding escape room. They would be locked in a cannibal serial killer's cold, concrete basement, and would have to figure out a way to escape before he came to kill and then cook them with fava beans and chianti.

After that, some sort of augmented reality gaming adventure. Orin liked the one with robots.

It was only after Dennis was signed up for the events, and Orin was deep into his game, when he saw the cost and realized there was no way he could sign them up for both. Same as BlastZone, neither came with a voucher.

"Can you pause that for a minute?"

"Dad, you're standing in front of the screen. I can't see."

"That's why I asked you to pause. Please."

Orin grumbled, dramatically thrusting his body to the side in a pantomime of trying to see around his father. "I can't pause a live game. Unless you want me to die."

"We wouldn't want that," Dennis said. "Just give me a minute before you start the next game."

No response. Just Orin still working hard to see the screen.

"Orin?"

"Okay. Sure. I'll call you over before the next game."

DENNIS WOULD'VE bet both balls in his sack that Orin started another game before calling him over. It wasn't worth the argument. He couldn't wait through another round. But then Dennis saw him starting what was at least the third game, and had to stop him.

"Remember what you said …"

"Oh right. Yeah. What do you need?"

"We'll have to pick between the escape room and the—"

"The escape room is fine."

Fine by Dennis. The escape room was two-thirds the number of credits, and he'd already spent a lot more than he had on the training challenges to help them prepare for the Millennial Knight. They would have to start using the vouchers; these bonus activities were killing him.

"Can I start the next game? Everyone is waiting on me."

"Almost. I also signed us up for some outdoor challenges. They'll help us to—"

"Wait. So we're not doing the VR stuff, but we're going to go on a bunch of hikes?"

"I don't think we're 'going on a bunch of hikes.' We're training together, so we can kick the Wilders' asses. Isn't that what you wanted?"

"Actually, I wanted to have fun, assuming we have to do this at all. BlastZone was a good time. Why can't we just do that again?"

"We did it last week."

"So?"

"So, famili only counts it once."

"Oh, right. I can see how that matters."

"You know it matters if you want to win, Orin."

"Let me get this straight … we can't do the VR Adventure, because we can't afford both a robot adventure and the escape room, but we're doing some training course that probably costs a lot more?"

"We already paid for the trails when we signed up," Dennis explained. "It's part of the training. How are we supposed to beat the Wilders, or win prizes, if we don't do the challenges ahead of time? That's what you said you wanted."

"I'm okay without winning any prizes, Dad. I just want to have fun."

"The training course will be fun."

"The VR robots will be funner."

"*Funner* isn't a word. Don't you want to kick Ryan's ass? Phoebe's watching."

"You shouldn't have asked me what I wanted if you weren't going to let me choose. The training course is going to be a lot harder, and less fun."

"I'm sure you're right about the first part," Dennis said. "But definitely not the second. We'll have as much fun as we decide to. So can you please be excited with me?"

"About a training course that sounds like it's filled with exercise that I'm probably going to hate?"

"No pain, no gain." Dennis tried to smile, but it was getting harder.

"Everyone is waiting on me to start the round."

"Maybe they should play a round without you."

"I'm the best at spotting the snipers."

"Then they'll probably appreciate you a lot more once you're back in the game."

"Dad …"

"I'm serious, Orin. Put down the controller and give me your attention for a few minutes. Then you can go back."

"*Fine.*"

Orin threw the juke controller, hard enough to crack the plastic, if it had landed on the hardwood floor instead of the sofa.

"Our training course starts on Sunday morning."

"This Sunday?"

"Yes. This Sunday."

"How early?"

"I'm not sure. Early. Probably five. We have to drive a bit."

"FIVE?"

"Yes, Orin. Five. We've done it before, we can do it again. Remember all our time in Scouts?"

"How could I ever forget, with you constantly reminding me?"

Dennis sighed, then sat on the sofa next to Orin. "Come on, man. I know you're almost sixteen, but that doesn't mean you have to turn everything into a battle. This will be exactly as fun as you decide. So can you please choose to care a little more, and make it more fun for both of us?"

To his surprise, Orin seemed to soften.

"Sure, Dad." He gestured at the tablet. "I assume you want to show me something."

Dennis handed the tablet to Orin. "I thought you'd like this."

"What is it?"

"It's all getting delivered tomorrow," Dennis said, wanting Orin to see for himself.

He studied the screen, his face lighting up.

"So what do you think?" Dennis asked.

"Mom's not going to like this."

"Then maybe you shouldn't tell her." He gave his son a mischievous grin. "To be clear, I'm not telling you to keep secrets, I'm just saying you're old enough to decide what you want to share."

But Orin wouldn't say a word. Dennis had ordered everything they might possibly need, and a couple of things they absolutely would not. Backpacks stuffed with survival gear. Compound bows with real arrows. Throwing knives and ninja stars. Not that they needed those, but Dennis overheard Orin telling his friend they were cool, and that he might want to take a martial art.

"Okay, that's cool," Orin said, handing the tablet back to his father. "Can I play now?"

Dennis pulled something else up on his tablet, then showed him the screen. "I have our old scouting manuals.

The course we'll be doing is comprehensive, but I thought it might be good to familiarize ourselves with—"

"You promised I could play again after I listened. The round is almost over."

"That was fast."

"Yeah. The team has a hard time staying alive when they keep getting pegged by all the snipers."

It was disappointing that after all the money Dennis spent on gear and opportunities, Orin still preferred to play a stupid game with his friends. He kept telling himself the same thing he'd been repeating like a mantra in his mind ever since last week.

Rebuilding my relationship with Orin is a process, not an event.

Last weekend was better than he expected. The same would be true for this one, but Dennis had to be patient, and give things a chance to unfold as they were supposed to.

"Sure, I get it. You can go ahead and play. Just one picture showing the gear we just ordered, so I can post it to our famili page. Okay?"

"Fine."

But it didn't look like Orin thought it was fine at all.

They forced their smiles, and Dennis took the selfie.

"Have fun," he said, but Orin didn't answer back.

He went to the kitchen table and looked through the burst. The pictures all seemed strained, but after around five minutes of deliberation, Dennis settled on the best one, figured not every pic could be perfect, and that really, perfection wasn't even the point.

The photo proved what it was supposed to, that Dennis and his son were doing this together.

Phoebe would see it, and so would @hawtestmom.

He posted the picture, along with caption, *Team Hoke is ready to kick some butt!,* hoping that Orin would see it later and finally get the gravity of what they were trying to do.

The earlier they attracted fans, the better they would do in the games.

Orin could have tonight, so they could share a better tomorrow.

And the rest of their perfect weekend together.

Chapter Seven

DENNIS ROLLED OVER, grabbed his phone from the nightstand, and hit snooze for the final time.

Or at least that's what he told himself.

Same as he'd been telling himself for the last half hour.

Just five more minutes, six times in a row.

But now he had to get up.

Dennis wanted to be ready to go, with pancakes on the table by the time he woke Orin at five, but he just couldn't do it.

Now he was disappointed with himself. Waking up to a pleasant aroma was so much better than opening your eyes to someone shaking you by the shoulders into reality. But taking into account of how slow he was going, and knowing that Orin probably stayed up at least an hour or two past when he promised, they would be lucky to throw on their clothes, get out of the house, grab some grub on the road, and make the training on time.

"You have to wake up," Dennis whispered to Orin, gently shaking his shoulder.

"Grmblerumrm," Orin said, turning over and putting the pillow over his head.

"We've gotta go."

"Blmbrmrmbrargr."

"If we don't leave in a few minutes, we're going to be late."

No response.

"Orin …" Another shake. "You have to get up."

Still nothing.

So Dennis went and turned on the light.

"Dad, what the hell?" Orin yelled, suddenly sounding very much awake.

"I'm sorry, but we really have to go."

"Why? Can't we just skip this one?"

"No. It's the first one. And I've already paid."

"The VR Adventure starts at noon," Orin grumbled.

"Five minutes," Dennis said, then left the room, intending to return in two minutes, sure that there was no way Orin would be up.

But he was wrong.

Orin was already getting dressed by the time Dennis was back. Nowhere near a good mood, but at least ready to go.

"Good morning again," Dennis tried.

"Whatever," Orin said.

Dennis already had their bags loaded into the car. They piled inside and hit the road, driving manual so the vehicle would allow its driver to go twenty miles per hour over the limit.

"How fast are you going?"

"Not that fast."

"It feels fast. Do you have any idea how much a speeding ticket costs?"

Dennis turned to his son. "Do *you* have any idea how much a speeding ticket costs?"

"I should. Mom tells me every day."

The answer surprised him into a laugh. "Well, she's right. They're a lot. After the cars all went autodrive, it became easier to prove intent."

"So shouldn't you slow down?"

"I'm just trying to catch up. We're late, and we can't miss orientation."

"A few minutes aren't going to matter, Dad."

Dennis shook his head. "You're wrong about that. A few minutes will totally matter. You should have seen all the big red alerts on the famili app about not being late. The last reminder I got when checking this morning said we'd be refused admission if we arrived after the appointed time. The app knew that we hadn't left yet."

"Does that mean I can't eat until we get there?"

"There are some protein bars in the bags. Just eat one of those."

"That's not breakfast."

"We didn't have time for breakfast."

"So you expect me to perform on some sort of obstacle course without even eating? What about breakfast being the most important meal of the day?"

"I told you, eat a protein bar."

"You're going faster than the speed of light. Shouldn't we be able to stop at a drive-thru, somewhere fast? It's early, so there won't be a line."

"If we see a place on the way, and there's no line, and we've made up our time, then yes. We can stop somewhere fast and grab something to eat on the way."

Fifteen minutes later they were a full four minutes ahead of schedule, just in time for Orin to spy a Sloppy's sign on the side of the road. One of their drive-thrus coming up in another ten miles.

"No," Dennis said.

"Why not?"

"Because that food is garbage."

"So. It's delicious."

"It's not delicious, your brain just thinks it is."

"What's the difference?"

"Your mother will kill me." Then again, "No."

"It'll be fast. There won't be a line this early."

"Sloppy's always has a line."

"How would you know? I thought the food was garbage."

"It is. That doesn't mean I never eat it. Sometimes I'm in a hurry."

"We're in a hurry now … you realize you're totally contradicting yourself, right?"

"I told you. Your mother will kill me."

"I thought it was cool not to tell her stuff now. If I can keep our weapons a secret, I can do the same for a trashy breakfast."

"They're not weapons, they're hunting tools. And I didn't say it was cool to keep secrets."

"Uh-huh."

Five and a half minutes ahead.

"Fine. We can stop at Sloppy's. But if there's a line we'll have to get back on the road."

"There won't be a line."

Orin was right. The drive-thru was empty. Dennis pulled up to the speaker and rolled down his window.

"Welcome to Sloppy's! Would you like to try our Incredibly Delicious Burger? It's incredibly delicious!"

Dennis wrinkled his nose. Who in their right mind wanted to eat a burger like that before six in the morning?

"What do you want?" he asked Orin, before turning back to the window. "Do you have anything for breakfast?"

"Of course! We have the Farm to Car, Bacon and Egg Ultimate Breakfast Sandwich."

Farm to anything was ridiculous when it came to Sloppy's, but Dennis just wanted someone to hand him a bag of food, so they could get the hell back on the road.

"Well, that's a mouthful. We'll take two of those."

"Would you like home fries with those?"

"I want an Impossibly Delicious," Orin said. "With regular fries."

"I'm sorry," Dennis corrected, "can we please get two Impossibly Delicious burgers instead."

"Of course! Would you like The Ultimate Experience with that?"

"No thank you."

"Yes!" Orin exclaimed.

"Fine," Dennis said to the speaker box. "Both with the Ultimate Experience."

"Of course!"

The girl sounded like a robot. He wondered if Sloppy's required her to start every sentence with an overly excited *Of course!*

"If you can please pull ahead to the parking area, we'll bring out your food as soon as it's ready."

"What do you mean?" Dennis asked. "Isn't it ready in like sixty seconds?"

No *Of course!* this time.

"Sorry, sir. It's the morning crew, and Jesus is new on the grill. He's still in training. It'll just take a couple of extra minutes, and we'll want to keep the line moving."

Dennis looked into his rearview mirror, saw no one behind him, and turned back to the speaker. "Sure."

"Will that be digicoin or credits?"

"Credits, please."

"Of course! Just wave your phone in front of the speaker to pay, then if you can please pull ahead to the—"

"I got it," Dennis said. It was too early for this bullshit.

Eight minutes later, Orin was on his phone and Dennis was fidgeting, about to go out of his goddamned mind.

"Chill out, Dad. It's going to be fine."

"It's not going to be fine if we have to forfeit this morning, just so we could get some crappy food we shouldn't even be eating."

"We need breakfast."

"We have protein bars."

"They're not going to forfeit us, just because—"

"They *are* going to forfeit us, Orin. That's the whole point! Why aren't you getting it? We need to go."

"But we already ordered our burgers. We need to eat."

"A couple of minutes won't make a difference. We can make it up on the road."

"You mean *I* can make it up on the road!" Dennis snapped. "First of all, that isn't the kind of attitude that's going to help us win. And second of all, hauling ass on manual is a lot harder than you think. We need to—"

Dennis stopped talking when he saw the girl standing on the other side of the window.

He rolled it down and held his hand out for the bag, scowling.

"Sorry about the wait, sir," she said brightly.

He grabbed the bag. "I know you're probably trying, sweetheart, but you're going to have to try harder. People don't come to a shit hole like this to wait. They come to get fast crap. If I wanted to wait fifteen minutes for my food, I sure as hell wouldn't want to be eating trash. Do you understand me?"

"Of course!"

Dennis started to roll up his window, needing to get the hell out of here.

Halfway up, Orin shouted through it. "Sorry about my Dad, he's not used to waking up this early!"

Dennis pulled out of the spot, glaring at Orin, then peeled out of the parking lot and back onto the road.

"You do realize you just cut off that car."

"It's still kind of dark, and hard to see," Dennis said.

"Sure, Dad."

The rest of the ride was silent. Dennis sped faster than he had at any time since his license was new, praying he wouldn't get pulled over, or that the car wasn't sending the morning's driving data to his insurance company.

But every minute on the road, Dennis recovered more time, and began to feel a bit better. He thought about yesterday, and how great things had gone.

Their gear had come in early afternoon, and Orin had fun pretending to shoot things with the arrows. They went through their packs, and inspected every bit of their gear. It felt like the old days, back when they were in Scouts. No arguments or discord. Dennis didn't even mind that Orin wanted to play *HardCorps* with his friends after dinner. They had all Sunday to bond, and besides, he wanted to check out the famili app.

Dennis wanted to do some investigation, see who had won in the past, and how they claimed their victories. He also wanted to look into Team Wilder even more than he had been.

Those rabbit holes went deep, and it wasn't long before he found himself clicking every possible link, out of the famili app and over onto LiveLyfe. Dennis told himself he was inspired rather than envious, and that tomorrow would be his chance to start building the same thing with Orin.

Their car kicked up dust in the wilderness center parking lot with three minutes to spare.

"We made it!" Dennis yelled.

"I told you we would," Orin said, clutching his stomach, and looking a little green.

Whether the queasiness was from Sloppy's, his driving, or a blend of the two, Dennis had no idea. He hadn't been able to take a bite of his burger, though he filled up on fries, which were easy to munch from the bag.

Dennis got out of the car, went to the trunk, pulled out their gear, dropped Orin's in a pile, slung the slightly larger of the two packs over his shoulder, alongside the quiver already on his back, grabbed his compound bow, and turned to his son.

"Are you ready?"

Orin was holding his bow and his pack, also wearing the quiver.

"Of course!" Orin laughed, imitating the girl at Sloppy's.

"Smile," Dennis said, whipping out his phone for a selfie.

"Come on, Dad. You said we had to hurry."

"We do, but there's time for a photo of our father-son team, about to start our survival training."

Orin audibly grumbled, but he wasn't going to argue. Instead he pasted a phony-looking smile on his face and did a thumbs-up gesture, good enough for now, and Dennis shot the picture.

They trotted over to the waiting group as he uploaded it to the famili app, with the caption, *Barely made it, after our champions breakfast, but we're here now!*

Orin was obviously annoyed with him, but that was him being a teenager more than anything. Once the games were going and they were back to having fun, he would see that his father had done everything he was supposed to. Made sure they were both up early, stopped for breakfast, and hauled ass hard enough to get them there in time for—

Dammit.

As they approached the group, already doing pushups in the clearing, Dennis could see Team Wilder at the edge. Tom looked up, mid-pushup, saw Dennis, and gave him a cheery wave with one hand while the other stayed planted on the ground.

The instructor, a man who must've been six and a half feet tall, with the torso of a bear, yelled at the Hokes. "Nice of you to join us. Now drop and give me fifty like everyone else, and you can add an extra twenty-five for being the last ones here."

"But we're not late," Dennis protested.

"On time is late, and early is on time. Now I wanna see a hundred and fifty pushups between the two of you — NOW!"

Dennis slung the backpack off of his shoulder, but the instructor barked again.

"I didn't say you could take that off!"

He looked around. No one else was wearing their gear.

Dennis settled the pack on his back, finished the first agonizing pushup, and realized with a knot in his stomach, he wasn't ready for this at all.

But he sure as hell hoped that Orin was.

Chapter Eight

DENNIS HAD no idea what the instructor's real name was, but he went by Goliath, and that seemed so apt that he couldn't imagine the man going by anything else.

After a morning of brutal sprints, obstacle courses, attempts at throwing axes at targets, rowboat races, and other activities which Dennis felt far too old and out-of-shape for, Goliath finally called a break for lunch, about a half hour after Dennis seriously thought he might die. Everyone started breaking out blankets and coolers, as he increasingly felt like an idiot.

"You're serious?" Orin said, looking at his father with drooping shoulders and disappointed eyes. "You didn't bring *anything* for lunch?"

"We have protein bars."

"That's not lunch. Why didn't you bring lunch?"

"I thought we would all be eating together; that's what it said on the app."

"Yeah, Dad. It said we would be eating together, not that lunch would be provided. I barely even looked at the thing and you were staring at it all day, so why do I know that and you don't?"

A good question, and Dennis didn't know. He messed up, and now everyone knew it, especially Team Wilder, who were trying a little too hard not to notice.

"It's no big deal," Dennis said, trying to assure him. "We don't need a big spread, we just need a little fuel to get through the next half of the day."

In truth, Dennis spent most of the morning feeling like he might throw up, envious of Orin and his youthful stomach that processed a garbage burger and fries without any problems. The kid barely seemed to be breaking a sweat, while Dennis felt disgusting from whatever preservatives were laced onto his fists full of fries.

"Chocolate chip, or peanut butter?" Dennis asked, holding them both out for Orin to choose.

"Hmmm … do I want to be starving, or starving? I guess I'll go with chocolate chip."

Dennis handed his son the protein bar, trying to ignore the snipe, while feeling like the world's worst father.

He was swallowing his last bite as Wilder approached them. His son was nowhere in sight.

"Hey there, Dennis! It's great to see you out here. Hell of a challenge, isn't it?"

That was just one of the approximately 847 things Dennis couldn't stand about the guy, the way he would say something like *Hell of a challenge, isn't it?*, when what he really meant was, *What do you think you're doing, trying something this ambitious, and obviously out of your league?*

Dennis thought of what his father would say in this situation, then let the same words fall out of his mouth. "No pain, no gain."

Wilder laughed. "Couldn't agree more. Ryan and I just got back from Red River Gorge in Stanton, Kentucky."

"Oh yeah?"

"Yeah!" Then he continued, as if Dennis had asked. "Place is gorgeous. The climbing is great. Permanent anchors and bolts. Close together if you want them to be. A bunch of routes, and experience levels. Even for beginners. You and Orin should try it."

"We'll look into it," Dennis said, wanting Wilder to go the hell away.

"I've gotta show you the pictures we shot from the top. The view is incredible."

His offer sat at the very bottom of a long list of shit Dennis never wanted to do, looking at gorgeous pictures of exotic locations he'd never be able to afford or visit, that Wilder had already scratched off his bucket list.

He forced a smile. "Yeah, we'll have to do that sometime."

Wilder pointed toward his blanket, and Dennis finally saw Ryan, sitting in the lotus position while waiting for his father. "Looks like you haven't started to eat. We're right over there, if you'd like to join us for the rest of lunch."

Dennis was about to decline, but Orin opened his big mouth instead.

Speaking to Wilder, while glaring at his father, he said, "We didn't bring any lunch."

Dennis could feel himself flushing, his body at least ten degrees hotter. But before he could so much as stammer, Wilder was clapping a hand on his shoulder.

"That happens to all the newbies. Come on, we have plenty."

He turned and walked toward his blanket. Orin followed, and after a painfully reluctant moment, Dennis sighed and did the same.

Wilder wasn't kidding. Their spread was impressive, not just abundant, but also delicious. Dennis thought he was doing well by ordering two types of protein bars to give Orin a choice, but the Wilders had four kinds to choose from. In addition, they had several kinds of sandwiches, sliced cheeses, a giant bowl of fruit, pieces of dark chocolate, some sort of super healthy organic cheese puffs made from cricket protein, green drinks, and juices. Enough food to feed several father-son duos if he wanted. Asshole would probably get credit for that too on the app — Most Generous Father-Son Duo.

It all made Dennis want to crawl into a hole, and that was before Wilder took out his phone to bore him with an endless parade of photos he couldn't care less about while their sons excitedly chatted about *HardCorps*.

Due to circumstance, Orin was now forced to consort with the enemy.

But that's where they were, and Orin was shoving so much food into his mouth, Dennis had no choice but to sit there and take it, feigning interest, politely nodding while eating Wilder's food, wishing he didn't feel so damned resentful of the asshole who paid for his lunch.

Dennis the loser didn't think to bring anything more than a couple of boring protein bars. It was the perfect analogy. The best thing he brought was the worst thing in Wilder's entire spread.

As their break was ending, and the slideshow was mercifully over, Wilder insisted that they all take a picture — Team Wilder and Team Hoke — hanging out and having fun together.

This must be how Orin usually felt. Dennis couldn't wait for the photo to be over, smiling through gritted teeth, and annoyed that his son seemed happy. Not with him, but with the family they were supposed to be besting.

Wilder uploaded the photo to the famili app with the caption, *Two teams enter, one team leaves — who will win?*

He sent a copy to Dennis and encouraged him to post it as well. Dennis did, as though he needed the reminder. But by the time their cooler was neatly packed, he was even more agitated. Wilder's photo already had several hundred likes, while Team Hoke's had only three.

"We all ready?" Then, without waiting for an answer, Goliath bellowed, "Follow me!"

He led them into another clearing, where a dozen bales of hay were arranged in a row about a hundred feet out. A target hung from the front of each.

"The rest of the afternoon will be a crash course in archery. Pay attention — these rules will keep you safe."

Point arrows toward the target once they are nocked onto the string.

Shoot at the same time and in the same direction as the other archers.

Wait until everyone has finished and I give you the all-clear order before approaching the targets.

Under no circumstances should you remove your arrows from the target until I have given you the okay.

Running with arrows is forbidden.

As Goliath droned on about archery safety, reminding them all that failure to follow the rules was grounds for termination of the training, and their associated famili accounts, Dennis looked over and saw the Wilders attentively watching.

While Orin was barely paying attention.

Goliath finished his speech and everyone scattered.

The energy was nervous as the initial archers in line began nocking their bows.

Dennis pulled out his phone, wanting another picture. Something better than that last awful one with the Wilders that he had no control over.

They were third in their line, with no one behind them,

so Dennis pulled Orin to the side and said, "Let's take a quick pic."

"No, Dad. Not everything needs a picture. Let's just stand in line and wait for our turn."

"Come on, you know how this works. If we post a picture now, we'll get a few extra likes, and that will help with our overall score."

"No," Orin repeated.

But Dennis already had his phone out. He might as well take advantage of the shot. What else were they going to do while waiting for their turn?

He tried to line up the shot, getting both himself and Orin in the frame.

"Stop it, Dad!"

Orin said it loud enough to embarrass him, probably on purpose.

But even worse, he said it loudly enough to invite ire from Goliath.

The instructor marched over to the Hokes.

"Doesn't sound like you two are taking this very seriously." He held out his open palm. "Now how about you hand over that phone, and give me twenty-five pushups each."

It wasn't a question. Dennis set the phone into Goliath's hand.

But Orin said, "It wasn't my fault. My dad is the one who wanted—"

"And you can give me an extra ten for throwing your teammate under the bus. Ain't you ever heard of solidarity?"

Dennis dropped to the ground and started his pushups.

Orin's palms were on the dirt a second later, as he threw his dad a dirty look.

I hate you, it said.

Dennis finished his pushups and waited.

But even after he stood, Orin refused to look at his father. Instead, he moved closer to the Wilders. He wasn't in their row, but it was almost as if he wanted the world to believe he was on their team.

With the more grueling part of their day finally behind them, Dennis felt grateful.

Archery was perfect. Goliath lectured, telling everyone what they would be doing, demonstrating the techniques, before taking a step back so others could try it for themselves.

How to hold the bow, how to grip the arrow to quickly nock it, and how to aim.

It all seemed simple enough. But when it was finally his turn, and Dennis had the chance to prove he could shoot, his muscles were shaky, weakened from the morning's exertion.

He shot six arrows, but couldn't hold his bow still enough to hit the target even once.

And to his surprise, Orin had the hang of it fast. He didn't land a single bullseye, but he hit the paper target every time. Dennis kept trying to catch his eye, let him know he was proud, while also quietly begging for his forgiveness.

But Orin kept looking away.

The lessons ended with Goliath telling the entire group that they needed to try harder, while appearing to speak to Dennis directly.

"In the next two and a half months, the true champions among you will transform yourself. You'll turn sit-ups into stomach curls, pushups into plank-ups, and jogging into endurance running."

Dennis hoped he wasn't going pale as Goliath finished his speech. This sounded awful, and much worse than what he meant to sign up for. But he couldn't let Orin see his dismay.

No matter how much of a problem he might have with the workout, Dennis had to keep that shit to himself. As leader of Team Hoke, he had to set the example.

"I suggest you all go home and rest. Don't do anything to tax yourself, even if the overachievers among you are tempted." And now it looked like Goliath was actively *not* looking his way. "You'll need the recovery time, even if you're not feeling it now. These weekend trainings will be brutal, but you'll need them to hone your skills. Stay consistent with your conditioning."

Goliath finished with another glance his way, Dennis felt certain. "Slack off and you *will* wash out."

The instructor thanked them, then turned his back on the group and went to gather his stuff. As timid as he felt having to approach Goliath to get his phone, Dennis was also glad for the distraction, and an excuse to avoid the Wilders.

"I'll be right back," Dennis said to Orin.

He walked over to Goliath, faking his confidence more with every step.

"Um, excuse me, sir?"

The instructor turned, saw Dennis, and looked like he had to stifle a laugh. "Yeah?"

"Sorry to bother you, but I was hoping I could get my phone." Dennis held out his hand, but felt like he should maybe take a knee.

Goliath set it into his hand. "If you don't take this seriously, you're out of here."

"Yes, sir."

"You understand there's no refund if I kick you out?"

Dennis nodded. "I do."

"You're in a battle, son," Goliath said, even though

78

Dennis was the elder between them. "You're in a war with yourself. That's resistance making you run late, making your arm shake, making you want to take a picture instead of doing the work. The real you is a frightened little animal, shaking in a cave, wanting mama's milk, and to be patted on its furry little head. That sound about right?"

Dennis had no idea what he was supposed to say, but "Yes, sir" always worked.

"Fail that, and you don't got a chance at any of this. See you next week."

"See you next week," Dennis said, though Goliath was already walking away.

Orin had all of their gear by the car, but was waiting in front of the closed door.

"This car should know me by now and just open the door," he complained as Dennis approached.

"Your mother has Sensitive Home, right?"

"Yeah."

"So add it to the app." He took out his phone. "We should take a quick pic before loading up, anyway."

"Fine," Orin said, sounding like it wasn't.

Dennis went to grab their bows, wanting a shot with a nocked arrow.

"Come on, Dad. The bows are already put away."

Dennis probably would've pushed it, taken them out and stolen a shot anyway, but he felt sure that Goliath was watching. Could feel the instructor's gaze burning his skin.

So he shot a quickie instead, added the caption, *In a war with ourselves, and winning. #dothework!*, pressed *POST*, then dropped the phone in his pocket and loaded the gear into the trunk.

Dennis opened the driver's side door, and started to get in, pausing halfway into his seat as he caught a glimpse of Team Wilder leaving the grounds.

It had to be them, kicking up dirt in a four-wheel-drive AUTOnomous X.

Dennis felt an admittedly unreasonable flush of anger. "We're going to have to work a lot harder if we expect to beat the Wilders."

"They're already so much better than us," Orin said, climbing into the car. "What's the point?"

Another flush of rage, this one hot enough to scorch him. "They're not *better* than us, Orin. They're just richer. *We* deserve to win that prize."

"Whatever." Orin shrugged.

But that *Whatever* ate at his insides, all the way home.

Because if Orin gave up on Team Hoke, what did that mean for their relationship as father and son?

Chapter Nine

Dinner was decent, but nothing like Dennis had imagined.

He bought ingredients for one of the many recipes the app suggested parents use to cook healthy meals with their families. The kitchen was one of the best rooms in the house to bond with your teenager, or so said one of the 4,371 videos in the famili app library.

"Do we have to cook?" Orin had asked, obviously exhausted.

Dennis wanted to stand his ground, and tell him yes. But in truth he could barely lift his arms, let alone chop. Cooking sounded terrible, and nowhere near as enticing as ordering pizza.

And besides, if Dennis held his ground, it would be harder to insist that they watch a movie, after Orin got his hour of *HardCorps*.

He was smart enough to choose their battles. Meat lovers it was.

Now dinner was done with and Orin's hour already spent.

"One more game," Orin begged.

"You already had one more," Dennis reminded him. "Come on, it's time to watch a movie."

Orin looked up at him. He wasn't going to ask again, but the kid was still making his face as pathetic as he possibly could. A wounded puppy, starving for food and attention.

"Five minutes, then it's movie time. That gives you just enough time to get ready for bed. Pajamas on, teeth brushed. It's time for—"

"What am I, ten?"

Dennis waved a hand in the air. "You're almost sixteen, so what. You're gonna put on pajamas and brush your teeth, right? You think you don't need a reminder, I disagree. Your toothbrush is synced to the famili app, so I know about last night."

Orin flushed with embarrassment, but wasn't hostile back.

Dennis accepted it as a win.

Orin went off to get ready for bed while Dennis queued the movie. It was an older film, but his son had never seen it. He'd given the evening a lot of thought, and this was the perfect movie to share. There had never been anything like it. They could easily get the same actor to convincingly play any age these days, from five years old to a hundred. You couldn't tell the animated parts from reality.

But *Boyhood* was old school. Shot over twelve years. The actors kept coming back, and the director kept shooting one slice of his film at a time. It got robbed of its Oscar. Dennis had seen the winner a couple of years ago, and it just confused him.

Boyhood was special, the best movie about growing up ever made. They would sit on the couch together, watch a child age in front of their eyes from five years old to sixteen like Orin almost was now, to when the movie ended with Mason heading off to college, and staring into an unknown horizon.

They didn't make movies, or life, like that anymore.

"Ready?" Dennis asked when Orin emerged from the bathroom.

"If I have to be."

"Come on, a quick pic before we start the movie. You know, *Down with the classics.*"

"Please don't say that."

Dennis tried to take the photo, but Orin squirmed away. "Not now, I'm not in the mood."

"It'll be quick."

"I'm not really concerned about how long the embarrassment takes."

Dennis laughed. "Okay, I get it."

But he really wanted to take the picture.

Dennis started the movie.

But almost immediately, he could tell that Orin wasn't into it. He wasn't laughing at the funny parts, or smiling at much of anything. He didn't seem in any way impressed that Mason was growing up in between the scenes, right in front of his eyes, without the aid of special effects.

"How are you liking it?" Dennis asked, midway through.

"It's good," Orin said, sounding like he was lying.

"You don't like it?"

He shrugged. "It's okay."

"What don't you like about it?"

He tucked some hair behind his ear. "The dialogue is clunky."

"Oh?"

"And the acting isn't very good."

"Well—"

"I mean, the parents are fine, but it's all kind of flat."

"But those are the real kids," Dennis said, pausing the movie. "They had to come back every year, to show them actually aging."

"Why didn't they just use mocap?"

"They didn't have mocap back then."

"How old is this movie?"

"Well, they had it. But not like now. You couldn't have done this then."

"Maybe they shouldn't have."

"You don't like it at all?"

Orin smiled, what looked like an apology. "I bet it was awesome when it came out."

"But don't you get it?" Dennis really wanted him to get it. "This movie was made over eleven years. Every moment is fleeting, and feels heavier because of it. Don't you think that's interesting?"

"Yes. It's interesting."

"That sounds sarcastic."

"It's not sarcastic."

"Then why do you sound like that?" Dennis asked.

"Because maybe it's a waste of time."

"How is it a waste of time?" Dennis felt insulted, on behalf of *Boyhood*.

"*Eleven years?*"

"You're saying art isn't worth taking its time? That's a beautiful thing. You sound like your grandfather. He's the only person I ever met who hated this movie."

"I didn't say I hated it."

"Right. You said it was *interesting*."

"Maybe we should finish it," Orin suggested.

"It *is* interesting. Think about the trust the director had to have in his idea. The amount of faith it must've taken, to let the details of his story come over time."

"You shouldn't like something because of the idea. The movie should be good. With, you know, believable acting."

"But the characters aren't acting so much as behaving," Dennis said. "They're almost self-conscious. Because they're less like actors than people who keep meeting up to make this movie. Don't you think that's amazing?"

Orin clearly wished he did. "Sorry, Dad, the movie kind of sucks."

"You haven't seen how it ends."

"So let's finish it," he said.

But ten minutes later, Orin was snoring.

At least the app didn't know, famili was still logging their father-son time under the tag *watching a classic together*.

Dennis took out his phone, logged into the app, and saw that Team Hoke had gathered another fifty followers. A lot more than he expected, and it should have made him happy. But then he checked the Wilders, saw their totals, and wanted to chuck his phone across the room.

It would take a mountain of dinner pics and quiet moments to catch up.

If they wanted to win, Team Hoke would have to do something big.

Chapter Ten

SUNDAY AFTERNOON, and time for the serial killer escape room.

Dennis woke up sore and did his best not to say anything. But once Orin admitted that he was dying too, Dennis said it felt like he had the devil's piss in his veins.

That actually made Orin laugh, which seemed to surprise them both. And that made him laugh even harder. Dennis played it cool, laughing just enough. A breezy, beautiful moment. The kind *Boyhood* captured so well.

Maybe Orin was less mature than he thought. It hurt, because ever since the first time Dennis saw that movie, and was rejected by his father after wanting to share it, he had assumed that his own son would love it just as much.

Instead he felt his father laughing. The drunken chortle that usually got him drooling.

He had to ignore it. Be better than his father. There were plenty of movies that hadn't aged well. Maybe *Boyhood* wasn't as good as Dennis remembered, and Orin couldn't divorce his perspective. That was fair. But he wanted to talk about it at least, and would if he didn't have the feeling that it would only get them into an argument.

They were both beat to hamburger after yesterday's training under Goliath, and would have gladly stayed inside if Dennis hadn't already paid the registration fee. But there were no refunds or cancelations. If they failed to show up, it was credits down the crapper.

But at least they got to sleep in. They were barely functioning, thanks to a gallon of caffeine and plenty of ibuprofen.

"You got it?" The attendant explained the rules, but he mumbled in a low voice, and Dennis's headache had yet to leave the building. But he wasn't about to ask the guy to repeat it.

"Got it." Dennis looked over at Orin. The kid was wincing. "How you doing over there?"

"Still sore."

"So we're good?" the attendant asked, looking at the Hokes expectantly.

"We're good," Dennis agreed.

The attendant left, and locked the door behind him.

"So we're really in here now, huh?" Dennis looked around the room. "Come on, let's take a picture before the first puzzle. Caption, *We got this.*"

"That's okay."

"One picture."

"No thanks."

"Give me one good reason."

"Everything hurts."

"Exactly. I bet your face muscles are the only things that don't hurt right now. You can do it, think of Phoebe."

His face cracked, the smile almost there.

"She's leaving comments; you saw the one she left last night. *Nice shooting, Robin Hood!*"

His smile split his face wider.

"Grab me the foot, and you can hold Mr. Grumpy." Dennis pointed to a decapitated head, blood caked around its deep and weathered frown.

Orin laughed, said okay, handed out the body parts, and posed for their goofiest and most sincere picture so far. Caption, *Bloody good time.*

The day went downhill from there.

"This whole thing is stupid," Orin said a half hour later. Frustrated and red-faced, looking like he wanted to stomp off, or maybe hit something.

"We just need to slow down long enough to think it out. We're missing something obvious. It's like overlooking the salt."

"What?"

"Hasn't that ever happened to you? You're looking everywhere for the salt, but you can't find it. Then you call someone in and they see it immediately, right there in front of you."

"Um, no. I don't cook."

"Yeah, right. Well, it happened to your mother all the time."

"And you used to help her?"

"Yeah."

"So," Orin said, "where's the salt?"

"I don't know, but we're close."

"It doesn't feel like it … I've never been very good at this kind of thing."

"Me neither," Dennis admitted.

After the first two puzzles went relatively fast, this third was giving them both a headache. It had been ten minutes of feeling stupid, and every one mattered toward their overall score.

They were staring at what looked like a numerical code

scratched into the wall, ostensibly from one of the serial killer's many victims.

"Maybe it's Morse Code," Dennis suggested.

"It not Morse Code."

"How do you know?"

"Because it doesn't look anything like Morse Code. Don't you remember, from Scouts?"

Of course he did. Dennis was leading them down yet another rabbit hole. "Maybe it's one of those cyphers, you know where A=1 and B=2, you know what I mean?"

Orin looked at the scratches, then at his father. "Yeah, I know what you mean. Is that what *you* think it is?"

"No." Dennis shook his head. "Maybe the numbers add up to something."

"Yep," Orin said, sinking down to the faux basement floor, his back to the wall. "It equals us being done with this. I give up."

"You don't mean that!" Dennis said. "Of course you—"

"Wanna hint?" The attendant's voice crackled through the speaker.

"That's okay," Orin yelled up to the corner. "You can just let us out now."

"Yes, we'd like a hint!" Then to Orin, "We're already here."

"Everything hurts."

"Sounds like life," Dennis said.

"So, yay or nay on that hint?" the announcer asked.

"Yay," they said together.

Dennis smiled.

"Examine the trophy boxes."

"What trophy boxes?" Orin asked, but the announcer was already gone.

"Those." Dennis pointed to the metal shelves on the farthest wall. They were lined with heads, feet, limbs, and vials of saliva. Eyes, locks of hair, and underwear. Both genders.

On the middle shelf, both above and below all the more obviously garish mementos, there was a row filled with seven tarnished silver boxes.

Dennis walked over to the boxes, picked one of them up, opened it, and found several more boxes inside. He turned to Orin. "It's filled with more boxes."

"They have numbers. They're dated."

Dennis turned to the wall, saw the dates, then said, "I'll find the boxes!"

Once they knew, it took only seconds. Then the Hokes were looking at a locket with an image of an old-fashioned woman, appearing stern in a black dress that went to the top of her neck. The picture was lying atop a poem, hand-written on a tattered piece of paper.

Orin studied the locket, then looked up at his father. "You think it might be some sort of a key?"

"No." Dennis shook his head. "It's too small."

"Things are smaller than they used to be, grandpa."

"Screw you, kid. I'm not that old. Things aren't much smaller than they used to be."

"So, what's your idea?"

"I'm not sure," Dennis admitted, his heart beating fast as he snapped a clandestine picture, pretty sure that he'd just gotten away with the perfect crime. Orin wouldn't mind seeing the photo later, especially if it had a comment from Phoebe.

He stole a glance at the photo on his phone. Orin studying the clue like a little Sherlock Holmes. Dennis added a caption, quickly posted it, and returned to the action.

Then he looked down at the poem, realizing that it had gone from prop to genuine clue.

"This poem has the words *north* and *south*." He showed it to Orin. "I think we're looking for one of those locks where the combination is made up of directions."

He smiled. "Good job, grandpa."

"Stop calling me that.

"Sure thing, Abraham Lincoln."

Dennis wasn't even sure what that meant. But he laughed, and Orin laughed with him. The moment was nice, until the attendant ruined it.

"Sir, I'm going to have to disqualify you," the voice said through the speaker.

"Is he talking to you?" Orin asked.

Dennis shrugged.

"Yes, I'm talking to you. The dude who was supposed to leave his phone in the provided locker outside the escape room. The dude who didn't and is cheating."

"I'm not cheating," Dennis said.

"Dad?"

"I was just taking a picture." Dennis looked from Orin to the camera with an apologetic expression.

"Dad!"

"I didn't mean to—"

"Having a phone for any reason inside the escape room is considered cheating, and is grounds for immediate forfeiture of the gaming experience."

Was the attendant reading a script?

"You said 'grounds for.' Does that mean there's any wiggle room here?" Dennis felt hopeful. "Maybe I can set it here on this trophy shelf, and promise not to take any more pictures, or do anything else."

"I'm afraid it doesn't work that way."

Then the door buzzed, and kept on buzzing as Dennis

stood a few feet away, dumbfounded. It only stopped after Orin marched over, threw it open, and stomped out of the escape room and onto the other side.

Crap.

Dennis ran after him.

But Orin hadn't just left the escape room, he left the building entirely.

Dennis couldn't go that fast. He had to clear out his locker, assuming he didn't want to come back and pay for another entrance fee.

That hadn't gone nearly as well as he hoped. But there was a win, if they were both willing to see it. Dennis was looking at it now.

Sure, famili was logged into their activity, so anyone who looked would know they didn't finish the escape room. But it probably looked like they got kicked out, like a couple of cool kids. And the photo he managed to upload had already earned fifty-four smileys and more than thirty new follows, with the number quickly growing.

If all of that didn't make this okay with Orin, Phoebe's comment certainly would:

Did you do something naughty?

Then below her comment, another for Dennis, from @hawtestmom.

Like father, like son.

Maybe Team Hoke could catch up after all.

Phoebe wasn't the only girl. Not by far. The follows kept pouring in. Fast enough to keep Dennis crouched in front of their locker, wondering when it would end. There was a parade of cute girls, all Orin's age. Giving his son smileys, messaging things to each other like, *he's too cute; I called dibs!* and, *If he comes inside my room, I won't let him escape!*

By the time Dennis got into the car, Orin was furious.

Crossed arms and ankles, a curled lip he could feel like a sunburn.

"Seriously, Dad?" Orin wouldn't even look at him.

"The pic is doing great!"

"You can't stop taking stupid photos for even a minute!" Orin blurted, finally turning to face him, and clearly upset. "What's wrong with you? Now they're never going to let us back in!"

"Isn't the point of playing the game to get ahead? That's what we did, even if we didn't solve the puzzle."

"I don't want to do this anymore."

"What? You mean the escape room?"

"Any of it. I'm done. I don't want to do anything with the famili app anymore. I want to go home and play *Hard-Corps* with my friends."

"Wouldn't you rather be playing it in another three months on a brand-new juke, with a new game — no, make it two games — you want already installed?"

"Not anymore." He shook his head. "Not if it means all of this."

"All of this?" Dennis repeated. "Woe is me, Orin. Like you really have it so bad."

"I don't want to hear about how hard you had it growing up, Dad. It's all an exaggeration, or some misguided attempt to connect with me. But like you said, things haven't really changed."

"At least you have a father who loves you."

"And by love you mean abandon, then smother."

"That's not fair, Orin. I didn't *abandon* you then, and I'm not trying to smother you now. Your mother wanted a divorce. It wasn't exactly like I got say in that situation."

"You got plenty of say. You created the situation."

"It isn't that simple."

"Seems simple to me. Maybe it will seem simpler the second time. *I quit.*"

"I didn't raise you to be a quitter."

"No, you raised me to be a drunk ... before mom kicked you out ... in the situation you had no say in."

"You're not being fair."

"You already said that, and I'm not sure it was right the first time."

Dennis was furious. This was like arguing with Susan. And again, Dennis wanted to grab a handful of Orin's hair, and tug with all of his might. "I can't help who I was then. That's in the past, but we can choose to leave it behind us. We can decide that it's worth building something better, based on our current relationship. You just have to let me in."

"You mean, I have to let you document the moment."

"Orin—"

"Let me guess, it's not fair. And you think I'm the immature one."

Dennis had to stop talking. He could feel it frothing on his lips, the same thing his father would have said, telling him not to be such a little pussy.

"Look. Dad, I'm not a quitter, and I'm not quitting. At least not on myself. Just this stupid app."

"Okay, so we learned something. That's great. We need a recovery day after an intense workout. The escape room was stupid, too ambitious. How about we see a movie instead?"

"Take me back to your place," he said with no emotion. "Or I'm calling Mom to pick me up."

So with gritted teeth, Dennis started the car.

Chapter Eleven

It WAS two and a half months until the Millennial Knight Tournament, and Dennis was losing his grip.

Not just on the tree he could barely hold onto, and was about to fall off from, but everything.

At least Orin was still signed into famili, still willing to play the game for a little longer at least. Dennis had thought he was finished for sure.

Then, when his mother decided to keep him last weekend for Orin's sixteenth birthday, and their bond was temporarily broken, he figured that was it. Instead of getting three weekends in a row as expected, Dennis spent the last Saturday and Sunday missing Orin, and feeling sorry for himself. He'd wanted to go to the birthday party, but Susan didn't even invite him. Nor did Orin say a word.

But now they were back in training, climbing trees, with their ultimate foes missing from this weekend's experience. Tom had a business meeting in Singapore, and took his son with him. That was probably exciting for Ryan.

Dennis had never taken Orin to work. He probably got

all he would ever want by going in with Susan. She was more impressive, with her being a veterinarian, and Dennis just an assistant.

The Wilders' absence was a surprise to Orin. He hadn't been obsessively checking their profile on the famili map, or stalking them on LiveLyfe. It was humiliating, how often he looked, and how much Dennis cared compared to how little he should. He'd probably be doing better with today's training if he wasn't up until two in the morning, going back through the Wilders' feed, trying to assess what other ninja skills he might've mastered, beyond rock climbing and all the other bullshit he liked to brag about.

Every new find made Dennis feel worse about himself, worse about his relationship with Orin, and worse about their overall odds, in general, and specifically against the Wilders and their obnoxious levels of privilege.

They did a *lot* of stuff together, but even on his own, Wilder traveled the planet for work, tucking adventures into wherever he went. Whether at home or abroad, he was always "working on himself," and documenting the consistently impressive results.

Wilder had done a ton of whitewater rafting, Royal Gorge, Youghiogheny, and Colorado River in the last two years alone. There were more before that. He got private yoga lessons to accommodate his constant travel. He had a personal masseuse. And — for some reason this agitated Dennis more than anything — he swam laps at four a.m., to "start his day right," which he posted like clockwork most mornings after he finished.

It wasn't fair. Thomas Wilder wasn't better than Dennis, his resources were just so much better. The disparity sickened him, this father and son from the other side of the looking glass, everything always coming so much easier to them and their rich, perfect lives.

Dennis would be amazing too, if he had someone to shake his dick after every piss. But he didn't. Instead Dennis always did everything for himself. He never had a private trainer, which was probably why he could barely hang onto the goddamned tree.

Dennis lost his grip and crashed hard to the ground.

His fault for not paying better attention. He should have been focused on his grip, instead of fixing his attention on the Wilders. He needed to let that go, to be present here.

It was just so hard to ignore the inequity of it all.

Dennis was flat on his back, looking around, hoping that no one saw.

But of course a few people had, including Orin and their instructor, Goliath.

Dennis had looked forward all week to beating the Wilders, but now he was glad they were in Singapore. If they were here they would have seen him fall, and would probably laugh at him the whole way home. Like always, Dennis felt sure.

He spit out a mouthful of leaves, then picked himself up off the ground, ignoring the throbbing in his hip, dull like a bruise waiting to bloom, scrapes on one palm and the inside of his wrist, a sharp aching in his ankle that he prayed wasn't a sprain.

Dennis awkwardly smiled at Orin, hoping he didn't look nearly as pathetic as he felt, then limped to his backpack and sat on top of it, wincing as he felt a jolt of fresh pain from a splinter under his fingernail that he hadn't noticed before.

Dennis dug into his pack, pretending to search for something, it didn't matter what, while trying not to wither in shame.

Goliath looked like he wanted to roll his eyes or shake

his head, maybe tell Dennis to go the hell home. Instead he turned to Orin. "Your turn."

No surprise, he took to it immediately. And they hadn't even practiced. Young and spry, he clambered up the trunk like a well-trained monkey.

Dennis was the problem. He was doing an awful job of adapting, while Orin was doing great. Much better than Dennis expected after their discord a couple of weeks ago.

It was impressive, how well his son was adapting to the exercise. He was in much better shape than Dennis had given him credit for, or maybe it was the glaring contrast between them.

While Orin appeared to be improving, Dennis had devolved, doing even worse than he had that first week, which was really saying something considering he'd missed every arrow and performed miserably in the sprints and axe-throwing.

Dennis wasn't especially coordinated. Never had been. And he didn't even need his father around to hear the constant reminders in his head. But there was also the cumulative stress on his middle-aged body. Enough to make Dennis feel a decade older than he was.

But at least he was trying. A truth he tried to document whenever possible. Goliath made it clear that there were to be no selfies or pictures, yet Dennis still sneaked what he could. It was the only place he could effectively compete. For now.

He would have to get a shot of these wicked splinters under his nails. Caption, *Worth the pain!* He'd love to get video of Orin climbing the tree, but couldn't pull it off without being obvious.

"Like this?" Orin called down from the top.

Goliath nodded, gave him a thumbs-up, stole another

withering glance at Dennis, then called for a five-minute break.

Finally. He'd been waiting to get a moment alone with Orin all morning. They'd barely traded a word since getting out of the car. But he didn't come over, or look like he wanted to. Instead he was hanging around a cluster of chattering families. The odd man out by choice.

Dennis walked toward their bags. He'd pretend to dig for a protein bar.

Goliath cut him off a few feet from their backpacks. "Thought you'd have quit by now."

Dennis wasn't an idiot. He knew what the instructor had been thinking, but it still took the wind out of him, hearing it out loud and without a note of apology.

"I signed up with my son," Dennis said, trying to smile. "There's no way I'm letting him down."

Goliath stole a glance back at the tree, the one where Dennis had fallen off a few times in a row not ten minutes before. "I can refer you to a more basic course. Something that—"

"No." Dennis shook his head. "It has to be this one."

"Why?" Goliath asked, eyebrows raised and voice perplexed, clearly wanting to know.

"Because we're competing in the Millennial Knight Tournament."

"Yeah, I know." Then, his curiosity sounding more sincere than sarcastic, Goliath asked him again. "*But why?*"

Dennis glanced over at Orin. That was answer enough. Even if their instructor wasn't a father, of course he'd done his time as a son.

"There are easier ways to bond with your kid," Goliath said. "And by easier, I mean less likely to land you in the hospital with a shattered pelvis."

"I'll be fine."

The instructor shook his head. "I'm not sure you will be."

"I know what I'm doing."

"It's my job to make sure that you do."

"Are you kicking me out?"

"I'm sorry, but you're just not in good enough shape for this." For the first time, Goliath sounded like he felt sorry for Dennis. And that was somehow the worst thing of all.

"I'll do anything. Just tell me how I can get up to speed faster. I can train on my own. I have nights by myself, all week long." Then he went ahead and said it out loud, the one thing Dennis didn't want to admit, hoping against all odds that maybe Goliath would be willing to help him. In a whisper he added, "*I just don't want to embarrass my son.*"

Another sympathetic look, followed by a shake of his head. "It doesn't work like that. Training takes time."

"I understand that, but is there something I can do to make it take *less* time? Even a little."

"We're talking about muscle, and muscle memory." Goliath grunted. "No offense, but you don't got either."

The insults kept coming, but Dennis tried not to take them personally.

"So you're saying I just need to get stronger, and practice more, right?"

"Well yeah, but—"

"What if I went to the gym every day? What if I started lifting?"

"Unless you were doping up, too, I can't imagine it making enough of a difference. And that's a terrible thing to put your body through."

Dennis hated the idea of taking performance-enhancing drugs, but this would only be for a few months, so maybe the juice was worth the squeeze.

"How much damage would it do to my body if I took steroids, but only until the tournament?"

Goliath shook his head, looking at Dennis like he felt even sorrier for him now than he did before. "Man, you don't want to do that."

"Why not?"

Instead of answering, Goliath said, "You ain't gonna find greatness anywhere but inside yourself. Seems to me you're looking for a shortcut."

"But I'm not," Dennis insisted. "I'll do all the work. I just don't want to let my son down. Please, you're the only one I know who can help me. Unless I start looking around the—"

"You know the famili app has plenty of challenges that are less physical, more mental. You ever consider those? Might be more your speed." Goliath gave Dennis what appeared to be a genuinely kind smile. "Seems like a place where you might place at the top instead of the bottom, without having to try so hard."

The Wilders weren't competing in any stupid mental challenges, so Team Hoke sure as hell wouldn't be either.

"I've already paid the registration fee for the Millennial Knight. It's non-refundable, and honestly, I can't afford anything else. I'm a single father, and I've put all of my money into this."

Then, as the Hail Mary it was, he added, "And my hope."

Goliath stared at Dennis for what felt like the most uncomfortable half-minute of his life. It was almost as though the instructor was looking right through him.

"*Please.*"

He finally broke. "Talk to D.B. at High Performance Fitness. He'll hook you up. And you can go ahead and tell him I sent you."

Then Goliath turned from Dennis and bellowed to the group.

"Break's over! Line up. We're hitting the tree again — harder this time!"

Chapter Twelve

"You can do it!" Wilder yelled to Orin.

Dennis had lost count of how many times now he'd wanted to punch the asshole in his face. But this was probably the most irritated he'd been so far. It was one thing to yell like an idiot when his own son was crossing the bridge. He had no right, trying to parent Orin.

"Don't look down, son!" Dennis bellowed, definitely louder than Wilder, but also at a higher volume than any human needed in the middle of a forest.

Orin glared at his father, clearly annoyed, wobbling a bit on the bridge.

Dennis felt a twinge of guilt. He probably shouldn't have yelled like that.

Orin was obviously distracted.

Still, it was Wilder's fault for starting it.

They were at survivalist training, carefully walking across a rope suspension bridge, one at a time. The Wilders were especially annoying, with Tom acting like his son was a hero, the way he kept hooting and hollering, praising every little thing his child did.

Despite looking dangerous, the bridge was safe, and getting across wasn't that big of a deal.

Or at least that's what Dennis thought.

But now it seemed like Orin might be having a harder time than he'd imagined.

Team Wilder got from one end to the other like squirrels racing across a power line. First Ryan, then his father, both scampering from one end to the other as if they had their own rope bridges at home. They probably did.

And Dennis was having a hard time being the bigger man. His emotions were unreliable, and he had a hard time dimming his anger.

At Tom for trying to parent Orin.

At Ryan for being the perfect son who could do everything his daddy asked him to do, while making it look easy.

And at Orin for not appreciating how hard Dennis had worked, and was constantly working, to make things better between them.

This was all for Orin, and yet his son wasn't grateful at all.

Dennis couldn't be the only one on Team Hoke who was willing to sacrifice.

And yet, that's exactly where he found himself.

He'd even gone to see D.B. at High Performance Fitness. Gave the guy Goliath's name, hoping that would eliminate the need of his having to say it out loud. But D.B., which apparently stood for Darius Brown, made Dennis work for it, only giving him a bottle of what he called horse candy, after Dennis agreed to sign up for a year of Trim, a group workout that was apparently like being able to "afford a personal trainer, even if he couldn't."

Yes, he was taking steroids.

But it wasn't a drug, and nothing like drinking alcohol.

Nothing that violated his AA, at least not in his mind. That didn't mean he was eager, or even willing, to tell Susan. Dennis also didn't want Orin to know, and he sure as hell wasn't about to register his use in the famili app.

Yet, he was still convinced that taking the horse candy was the right thing to do. And with just two months until the tournament, it was also the *only* thing Dennis could do if he wanted to end this thing as a winner instead of as a loser.

The steroids, along with the daily classes at Trim that Dennis had been treating like a religion, were quickly making a difference. A big one, too. Dennis not only felt stronger, he looked it. He was not only more powerful in each of his workouts, he had the budding body to prove it. He'd started sleeping naked, because even in only a couple of weeks the pounds were melting off, and his muscles were more toned and getting tighter by the day.

Unfortunately, it also felt like Dennis was stuck at the edge of frustration. Pissed at the world, and constantly aroused. Everything either made him want to explode in anger, or fuck without mercy. And right now, standing on the loser's side of the rope bridge, waiting for Orin to finish making his way across it, Dennis was desperate for something to punch.

Preferably Thomas Wilder's perfect fucking face.

Orin's foot landed on the other side of the bridge. Everyone cheered, Team Wilder loudest of all. So Dennis cheered even louder.

"Your turn, candy cane," Goliath told him.

Dennis could both feel and hear his contempt. He hoped that Orin couldn't.

What had seemed so easy, suddenly wasn't.

Dennis gripped both sides of the bridge, feeling Goliath's gaze burning the back of his neck.

He made it three steps before slipping for the first time.

After his sixth step he stumbled, his foot sliding right off the edge of the rope. Dennis had to hug the guide rope, pulling it close, clinging for his life as it swayed and he slowly — embarrassingly — regained his balance.

But even though his start was unfortunately clumsy, Dennis quickly recovered. After that second stammering teeter, he found himself in perfect control, thanks mostly to his new upper body strength. The horse candy was apparently working as hard for Dennis as he had been working for himself.

"You got this!" Wilder cheered.

"Come on, Mr. Hoke, you're killing it!"

What a couple of idiots, cheering for the guy who was eventually going to beat them. And he couldn't even laugh about it with Orin, who refused to so much as look his way. He stood on the other side of the bridge, arms crossed, sending his empty stare into the forest.

Dennis had strategically positioned himself to go last, so he could learn as much as possible by watching everyone else go ahead of him.

He made it to the other side, congratulated by the Wilders but still ignored by Orin.

"That's time! I'll see you all next weekend. Until then, remember that this is where the change happens. True victory comes from knowing you'll try again, and try harder, because there are no limits on what's possible when you do the work." Goliath cast a glance his way — only a flash, but enough for Dennis to catch it — and added, "Without any shortcuts."

So the instructor thought he was taking shortcuts. Dennis didn't see it that way. In a way, this was his only chance. Dennis was investing everything in famili, and specifically the Millennial Knight Tournament.

They agreed that winning was important, same for showing up the Wilders. Horse candy wasn't for everyone, but it made sense for Dennis. At least for now.

Professional athletes and actors needed an edge. Their livelihoods were tied to their physical performance, their appearance, or both. And weird as it was, the same was kinda sorta true for Dennis right now. His livelihood wasn't tied to his strength, but his ability to keep up with the Wilders most certainly was.

Goliath could roll his eyes all he wanted, deride Dennis's decision when he had no other choice. But Wilder and his brat had been training for their entire lives, simply by virtue of all the things they had that the Hokes very much did not. Thousands and thousands of credits, and even more important, all the hours to spend them.

Dennis had been dying to reconnect with his son, and against all odds he finally had a chance. There was no way he would let it slip through his fingers.

Goliath saw it as taking a shortcut, but to Dennis, it was his only shot.

But now, regardless of how hard he was trying, things with Orin were slippery. Dennis didn't know when he should cling to what they had, and when he should probably let go.

Wilder was packing up his gear, without Ryan for once, leaving his son to fraternize with Orin. But for reasons Dennis didn't understand, Orin wasn't walking away from the enemy.

And he was actually laughing at something Ryan was saying.

Dennis would die if they were making fun of him. Probably not; as much as Orin was sometimes annoyed by his father (like every son in history), he would never do that. Not with Ryan Wilder.

But the boys were smiling, and if Dennis wasn't careful, a friendship might develop.

"You ready to go?" Dennis finally asked Orin, awkwardly, and only after standing off to the side for several long moments, awaiting acknowledgement.

"I guess," Orin said, before turning toward Ryan and saying goodbye with a friendly wave.

Orin wasn't exactly giving his father the silent treatment, but he also wasn't talking.

Things were off, and had been all weekend. Single-word answers, and a lot of speaking only when spoken to. That was the way it had been with his father growing up, not the way Dennis wanted it to be with his son. The car was too quiet. Autodrive was doing all the work, so he couldn't even pretend to focus on the road like his father used to.

They needed a change of environment. A space that wasn't about the famili app or the tournament, exciting enough to occupy his mind away from *HardCorps*. And ideally, a place his mother would never take him.

"Wanna go to Kitty Kat Bubbles?"

Orin whipped his head around, turning to stare at Dennis, probably trying to see if he was kidding. He waited a moment, then finally said, "That's okay. We can just go home."

"Are you serious? You've never been there, right?"

"I'm sixteen, Dad. When would I have gone there?"

"That's right, you are sixteen now. I might have taken you there for your birthday, but I didn't have you last weekend. It's all ages, you know. Some families even go there."

"I doubt that."

"It's true," Dennis said. "Come on, you've gotta be curious."

"Fine, Dad. Whatever."

Smiling, he gave their car its new destination. "You're going to have a great time."

"Have you ever been there?" Orin asked.

"Twice. But never with my son."

A half hour later they were being led to their table at Kitty Kat Bubbles, a quickly growing chain, offering scantily clad servers in tiny skirts and low-cut tops. Kitty Kat Bubbles divided cuisine into regions. Dennis went with Southern American both times he'd eaten there. Massive platters of brisket, pulled pork, hot links, brown sugar-crusted ham, baked beans, coleslaw, chicken fried steak. Pecan pie and banana pudding for dessert, of course. Kitty Kat Bubbles also had Italian, Mexican, Thai, something they called American Bar Food, plus a few other world cuisines Dennis couldn't remember. Diners sat in the region they wanted to order from, and while customers could order any type of food from any part of the restaurant, it was fun to play along, sit in the appropriate province, and enjoy all the servers outfitted to match. The chain's existence angered approximately half the nation, Susan included.

Orin chose Mexican. Their server arrived in tiny denim shorts, and an embroidered blouse a few sizes too small.

"So, just nachos to start?" Rosa asked Orin.

He nodded, still looking down.

Rosa smiled at him knowingly, gave Dennis a wink, then walked away from their table.

Dennis punched Orin on his upper arm, not hard, but enough to get his attention.

Orin rubbed it, acting like it was much harder than it was. "What was that for?"

"How are you ever going to get a girl if you won't even look her in the eyes?"

"I'm not trying to 'get' our waitress, Dad."

"You're going to be a man soon, son, act like it."

The words weren't even out of his mouth before they started turning his stomach.

He felt disgusted with himself. Those were the *exact words* his father used to say to him whenever Dennis got shy around girls.

But I'm not my father.

Dennis had to remind himself, because that particular echo was still ringing in his ears.

His father would never have maxed out his credit cards just so he could bond with his son. He wouldn't have a single follower if he was leader of Team Hoke.

I'm better than my father, Dennis told himself again.

Then again, and again after that.

"So, what are you learning about Team Wilder's weaknesses?"

"Uh, that they don't have any?"

"Oh. I just noticed that you and Ryan were talking. I figured you were sussing him out, you know, trying to—"

"Did it ever occur to you that we might be friends?"

Dennis wanted to say, *That's what I was afraid of,* but that wouldn't go over well. Not with Orin's current mood. But he also couldn't just let it go.

"Aren't we supposed to be trying to beat them? Don't you remember — the Wilders are our enemy, *especially Ryan?*"

"He's only doing all this competition stuff because his dad is making him. He wants to quit." Then, mumbling under his breath he added, "Same as me."

"What?" Dennis had to check his temper. "What do you mean? You want to quit?"

Orin shrugged. "I already told you that, you just didn't listen."

"I thought you were kidding."

"You *hoped* I was kidding."

"What about Phoebe? Do you really think she's into quitters? I was in high school too, you know, and girls definitely don't like guys who give up."

Orin looked upset, but he kept it to himself, and didn't say anything back.

Dennis was dying for their nachos. Anything would be better than this sudden silence. He drew a deep breath, then softly exhaled. He wanted to fight with Wilder, not his only son.

Dennis got an idea, pulled out his phone, and showed Orin their team profile. "Look, we're getting more followers all the time. And our social scores are ten points higher than theirs. Do you know why?"

Orin looked across the table at his father, his eyes insisting that he couldn't care less, and said, "No, why?"

"Because our followers are more active. We could hit the jackpot with this."

Orin shook his head. "If I want to quit, you can't stop me."

"You're right," Dennis said, tiptoeing his way through a field full of landmines. "I can't stop you. But the first place prize is ten thousand credits, plus a ton of other prizes we could never afford. Do you really want to quit on that?"

"Our odds suck. We'll never win."

"Not with that attitude. Come on, Orin. If there's even a chance you could say *yes* right now and change your life forever, don't you want to take it? There's no reason to quit."

Orin thought for long enough that the nachos were on the table by the time he seemed ready to answer. Rosa asked for their order, but Dennis wanted to know if she could come back.

There was a light in Orin's eyes, and something tugging the corners of his mouth into a smile. "Fine. But if we win, I get half the prize money. No putting it savings, or into my college fund. My half belongs to me, and you can't tell me how to spend it."

"Of course!" Dennis couldn't have been happier.

And apparently the same was true for Orin. He seemed almost instantly changed. Not only was he willing to take a selfie, this one was his idea.

When Rosa returned to take their order, he even asked her if she could get in the picture. She was delighted, of course. Anything for a bigger tip.

Orin smiled. "Say *queso*."

"Queso!" Dennis and Rosa both said.

Orin uploaded the photo himself with the caption, *Fueling up!*

Then they ordered more than they could possibly finish.

Dennis didn't even care about the tab, not now that Orin was playing to win.

Chapter Thirteen

DENNIS PUSHED his plate across the table, wanting it as far away as possible.

He couldn't eat another bite, and might explode if he tried.

Orin wanted Chinese, and Dennis wanted to get the kid whatever might make him the happiest. With only a month and a half left until the Millennial Knight, the promise of their ultimate adventure was finally being delivered.

Things between them were as shaky as that rope bridge. The perfect metaphor for this entire undertaking. Until a dinner that changed everything. Got them on the same side, once and for all.

Orin had been playing full out ever since, even responding to Dennis's messages throughout the week, which he'd mostly been ignoring before, or answering with an obviously begrudging reply.

But there was still so much work to do.

Until they won the tournament, there would *always* be work to do.

"Thanks for dinner, Dad."

Dennis didn't hear a note of sarcasm in Orin's voice. It sounded like he actually meant it. "So, are you ready to hit some of these comments?"

Orin shook his head. "I'm gonna play some *HardCorps*. Thanks, though."

"You can play once we're finished, right?"

"Or I could play now."

"But we have more than two hundred comments."

"That's awesome. Good for us," Orin said, with a hint of his retired mood returning. "But my friends are all waiting to play."

"They can wait until we're done. If we work together, it won't even take that long. We can split them in half."

"We don't have to reply to every comment, Dad. That makes us look desperate."

"No, it doesn't," Dennis argued.

And he had every right to. He had looked into this. Outside of the clinic, the tournament was his life. Navigating his way around the famili app was most of what he did during the week, while waiting to see his son on the weekend.

"Our audience engagement is the biggest reason we're catching up to Team Wilder. Answering a comment only takes a few seconds, but it makes our followers feel bonded to us. I know what I'm talking about here. If we can keep our fans excited until after we've won the tournament, we'll have the edge we need to—"

"Fine. Can we answer them tomorrow?"

Dennis shook his head. "Sorry, Orin. I know you want to get on with your friends, so let's get this done fast. But if we don't take care of this tonight, we'll have to do it tomorrow, in addition to all the new comments still coming in."

Orin looked at him without saying anything. Dennis could feel him wanting to argue.

Instead he surprised his father again. "Well then, let's get started."

They buckled down and got all of them answered in less than an hour.

"Aren't you glad that's done?" Dennis asked as Orin was booting up the game.

"Yep," he said, grabbing his controller and collapsing back onto the couch.

Their division was perfect, with Orin responding to any avatars that looked remotely close to his age, and Dennis taking all the rest.

And now with all of the basic comments answered, he could get to the main event.

As usual, some of the comments were flirty. There were always a few, but the number was constantly growing. Tonight it seemed to have taken a leap. In addition to the regular batch from @hawtestmom, who had taken to calling him SuperDad, there were now branches off of branches off of branches — new followers, all stemming from the @hawtestmom tree.

She had recruited a battalion of girlfriends from her book club, yoga class, and Taco Tuesday with the girls.

One of the comments even suggested that Dennis might like to leave his son at home one Tuesday night, and join the girls for *All the tacos he can eat.*

Double entendre aside, it seemed like the world was rooting for Team Hoke.

Orin was playing *HardCorps* when Dennis heard a knock on the door. Four times, before he realized it wasn't just another concussive explosion braying from the juke.

I'll get it.

But Dennis didn't say it, since that was only his father talking, anyway.

He looked through the peephole, and dammit, sure enough it was Susan standing on the other side of the door.

He opened it and said, "You're early."

She wrinkled her nose, almost imperceptibly, but Dennis knew her well enough. "What's wrong with you?"

"What do you mean, what's wrong with me?" Dennis opened the door wider and stepped aside to let her enter.

"Hey, Mom," Orin said, barely any expression, and without looking up from his spot on the couch.

Susan didn't answer, her gaze raking Dennis, and then his apartment before she repeated her earlier question. "What's wrong with you?"

"Why do you keep asking me that? Nothing is wrong."

"You look terrible, and you smell even worse."

Dennis laughed. "We were working out all day. Training. I haven't had a chance to shower."

She wrinkled her nose again, this time on purpose. "Can you smell yourself?"

"What do you want, Susan?"

"You're drinking again." A statement instead of a question.

Dennis went from lightly agitated to fully annoyed, a hair trigger away from irate. "I already told you, several times, I'm not drinking."

"Well, *something* is going on."

"Yeah, my ex-wife is here three hours earlier than she's supposed to be."

"Maybe that's because I have a few questions."

"Great. Why don't you tell me what they are so I can get you some answers, and then get you out of here. You're welcome to come back in another three hours."

But for some reason, Susan was staring past Dennis, looking into his apartment. She shook her head, gaze moving down to the floor. He expected her to say something like, *I'm welcome to come back whenever I goddamned want.*

Instead she said, "You're drinking again."

"Will you please stop saying that?" Dennis wanted to scream, almost did.

But then he turned around. And for the first time, he saw his apartment through Susan's eyes.

The place wasn't just filthy, it was an embarrassment. They had tracked mud and leaves everywhere. Stacks of dirty dishes and takeout containers, piled through the weekend, crowded on the dining room table, and scattered along the kitchen counter. Nothing in the sink or trash. Clothes were in piles, along with the assorted detritus, shed from their weekend like dead skin through the room.

It wasn't worth cleaning up. Not when there were pictures to post, comments to answer, and Team Wilder to troll on the famili app.

But Dennis now saw it as Susan must have. He'd probably think he was drinking too.

As if on cue, Orin's character exploded into a hundred bloody nuggets onscreen.

"Shit! Fuck!"

"What did he say?"

Of course she heard him, and Dennis didn't need to look around the room again to know what she was probably most fixed on. Orin's backpack, the only tidy thing in the room. Neatly zipped and sitting by the door, and judging by the environment, it was easier to believe he dropped it there on Friday night than had it ready to go three hours early.

"We need to talk." She grabbed Dennis by the arm,

yanked him into the hallway, and slammed the door behind them.

"What gives? I'm not in the mood."

"And you think I am?" she asked, both bitter and upset.

"I stopped trying to read your mind a long time ago. I found it to be a fruitless exercise."

"I'm taking Orin home with me."

"I appreciate that you have full custody, and have been granting me these weekends. Thank you. But if it's my time, then you have to let it be *my time*. You can't ambush me, then complain that the place isn't picked up."

"I don't give a shit that your place is messy, Dennis. I'm concerned that I'm seeing a pattern. It's hard for me to believe that you're not drinking, or using, or something. It's even harder for me to be okay with exposing Orin to that."

Dennis laughed, waving his hand in dismissal. "I told you, I'm not drinking. Or taking drugs, or anything else. You caught boys being boys, and believe me, it could be worse. This is no big deal, and honestly, it's good for him."

Susan shook her head. "I don't think it is. Did you know that Orin's grades are dropping?"

"How much are they dropping?"

Looking even more upset than she had a second ago, Susan said, "A lot."

Another wave of his hand. "It's just school. Not like that means what it used to."

"That's what I'm talking about! This is exactly what's wrong." Susan lowered her voice, even though the door was closed. "I found throwing knives and ninja stars in his desk drawer."

He smiled, then it broke into a laugh. It did look bad, if you didn't know what Dennis knew. As much as he'd wanted to keep their adventure a secret, until after they had won the title of this year's Millennial Knights, it was clearly time to confess.

She was looking at Dennis aghast, horrified by his laughter.

"I have something to tell you."

He caught her up on everything, starting with the training they'd been doing every weekend for the last couple of months, starting just before Orin's sixteenth birthday, covering the major highlights bringing them into the present, and painting it all with an honest, albeit flattering, brush.

"So, part of the tournament is being prepared for the unexpected, that means dabbling in a lot of different areas. Orin really wanted to do some martial arts, so I was helping him prepare."

"With throwing knives and ninja stars?" she shrieked.

He knew she wouldn't like it, but Susan was still making a much bigger deal about this than Dennis expected.

"And you thought this was a good idea?"

"Sure," Dennis said. "We haven't been this close in years."

"You're not supposed to be his best friend, Dennis. You're supposed to be his father! Did you know he's been caught skipping school? Twice now. With Ryan Wilder. Do you remember him?"

Dennis had to hide his surprise.

No, his shock.

"I understand where you're coming from. I'll talk to him, right now."

Susan went for the door. "I'm taking him home."

Dennis was starting to panic. He had worked too hard to lose it all now.

"You can't do this, Susan. Please."

"I would say the exact same thing. It's only been a couple of months, and you're already off the rails."

"But I'm not," Dennis insisted, shaking his head and losing a brittle little laugh. "Believe me, I get how this looks. But that mess in there is evidence of us having a good time. Bonding. I wanted to keep this all a surprise until we won, but seriously, Susan, you should see how much he's striving. He's totally taken to it. Climbing trees, crossing rope bridges, working on his strength, flexibility, and balance. Aren't you always saying you want him to get out into the world, and start doing real things, instead of playing video games all the time? That's what we've been doing."

"He's in there playing video games right now!" She jabbed her finger at the door. "And that's *HardCorps*, Dennis. I'm not stupid. He's not supposed to be playing that game at all!"

"He sixteen years old. If we don't let him play it, he's just going to play it with his friends and resent us for not letting him grow up. You know he was secretly playing it long before our first weekend together. The kid is a ninja. Are you really telling me you haven't seen any positive changes?"

Susan softened as his argument gained weight.

"The training's been good for him. He's—"

"I don't understand why you're doing this."

The moment apparently over.

"Doing what?" Dennis asked.

"Teaching him to be so competitive. That's what your father did to you, acting like winning is the most important thing, and you hated it. You swore you would never do that to Orin."

"I'm not."

"And I'll add, this is the kind of thing you do when you're drinking."

"I'm not drinking!" Orin yelled like a drunk.

Susan blanched.

Dennis reset himself. "Here, just let me show you something."

He took out his phone, opened the famili app, and swiped to their profile.

Then handed Susan the phone and let her scroll through the photos herself.

He watched her eyes as she swiped through the library, seeing photo after photo of their smiling son, doing all of the outdoorsy stuff she'd been wanting him to. Bonding with his father in a way he hadn't been able to experience in years. She probably saw all the comments, and smileys he was getting from girls his own age.

Dennis could read it in her expression. It was happening without her, and differently than she would have liked, but maybe that was okay.

She handed over the phone, her eyes glassy, a tear about to leak from her right eye. "Fine. I'll see you in a couple of hours. But I need you to talk to him, Dennis. You can't just be his buddy and leave me with all the heavy lifting, not—"

"I got it."

Susan looked at him, not quite believing, but clearly wanting to.

"I promise," he added.

"And one more thing."

"Yes?"

"No violence. Bows and arrows are fine, I guess, it's very outdoorsy, and he does look happy in those pictures, but I don't like the knives, and I won't tolerate any guns or—"

"I got it." Then again, "I promise."

Susan gave him a smile, filled with more understanding than he was used to from her, then promised to come back at her appointed time, and leave him alone with Orin until then.

Dennis went back inside, found Orin's attention still glued to the juke, looked around at his thrashed apartment, and heard Susan's accusations as they rattled around inside him.

"Time to turn the game off."

"Mom waiting to go?" Orin asked, without pausing or looking over.

"She'll be back in a couple of hours. You're going to help me clean up until then."

Orin gave him a loud, mocking laugh. "Sure Dad, that sounds amazing."

And then he kept playing.

"I'm serious, Orin."

"I bet."

"Your mom will be back here to get you in a couple of hours. She saw what this place looks like now, and I want her to be pleased with what she sees her boys have done when she comes to pick you up."

Orin dramatically looked around the apartment. "Rick here?"

A long lock of hair fell in front of his face, hiding his smirk.

"Why do you care what she thinks? You've never cared what she thinks."

Dennis wouldn't go back and forth. They had work to do, and Orin had some questions to answer.

He marched over to the juke, turned it off mid-game, waited for Orin to stop screaming at him, then held his eyes and spoke in his most level voice.

"I said we had work to do, and that you needed to turn it off."

Orin caught one look at his father's face, either remembered something from before the divorce or wasn't willing to test fate so late on a Sunday, and shut his open mouth. Then he stood from the sofa and asked Dennis what he wanted him to do.

"We can start with you telling me why you've been cutting school."

Orin looked surprised, but he answered without hesitation. "I needed archery practice." Then he used his father's words against him. "You do want to win, don't you?"

"With Ryan Wilder?"

"Who else am I going to practice archery with? His dad is making him do the stupid tournament, too. And he has an archery range at his house."

Of course he does.

Maybe Dennis was looking at this all wrong. Maybe Orin was being proactive, brushing up on his archery without Dennis having to spend any extra credits. Maybe he was the smart one, using Ryan without him knowing it, training in his home so he could eventually beat him.

Dennis took a photo — the *before* from their eventual *before and after* — then they started to clean. They were diligent, managed to make the place look presentable. But Orin stole glances at the juke the whole time, like an addict eyeing a pipe.

Susan had made some excellent points, and Dennis promised to be on it.

So when they were finished cleaning, with only a few minutes left until his mom was supposed to pick him up, and Orin begging to play just one more game of *Hard-Corps* while they waited, Dennis said, "No. Absolutely not."

He promised her no violence, and it was good for Orin to do without.

And Susan seemed pleased, looking around the relatively spotless apartment, and nodding with approval at the sleeping TV.

"Thanks," she said, and Dennis didn't hear a single note of sarcasm.

"Of course," Dennis said, meaning it.

Then he closed the door, pulled out his phone, and checked the famili app.

More comments. Dennis planned to answer them all before bed, but he might as well feed the fire. So he took a picture of his clean kitchen, only one room and from the angle that best obscured his poverty, then uploaded it with the caption, *Cleaning the cobwebs together!*

He was already on his way to the bedroom when @hawtestmom left a comment.

Her first DM.

Dennis opened the message, saw @hawtestmom's x-rated photo, then settled onto his bed to answer a comment like he never had before.

Chapter Fourteen

DENNIS LOVED SHOOTING a lot more than he liked to admit.

He wasn't technically lying to Susan when he agreed to no guns. But after Orin told him that target practice with weapons would give them a definite edge in the Millennial Knight Tournament, he finally relented. After Orin agreed that he'd never, ever tell his mother.

No matter what.

"How do you know it will be part of the contest?" Dennis had asked.

"Ryan's dad studies these things. It helps with the weight ratio, or something like that. So I really think we should practice."

It wasn't an answer, and Orin probably just wanted to shoot guns, but as much as he was loath to admit it, Wilder was a man who knew things like that. Why ignore his insight, when Dennis could use it to crush him instead?

The guns felt like a reward after Saturday's training. It had shredded them both, rappelling down cliffs. Dennis was grateful for the ibuprofen, the horse candy that helped to strengthen and tighten his muscles, and all that time at

Trim. The Hokes were mentally and physically prepared to compete.

Orin traded his rifle for the Glock, took aim, and emptied his magazine into the target.

His jaw was set, and eyes were determined, his expression unnaturally grim. Orin didn't seem to be enjoying the experience, so much as resolved to excel.

Dennis had to admit, all that time playing *HardCorps* was good for something. He'd displayed his prowess at BlastZone, but that all felt imaginary. Here he was, with actual targets, and Orin was hitting mostly bullseyes, shots clustered around the head and heart.

The kid didn't miss once.

But even with all the famili points to prove his excellent parenting, Dennis couldn't share their success with Susan. Unfortunately, she just wouldn't get it.

"Your turn, Dad."

Great. This hadn't gone well so far. As much as Dennis enjoyed watching Orin perforating the targets, he hadn't had nearly as much luck himself.

And sure, it was fun pulling the trigger, but Dennis had trouble keeping a steady hand. Probably the horse candy, it was fucking him up in more ways than one. He had acne for the first time since adolescence. Not just the little breakout like he sometimes got after eating too much ice cream, his back was peppered with pimples. The biggest ones were swollen with pressure. His skin was oily, and so was his hair. Clumps came out in the shower.

But it was fine, because this was all temporary. The Millennial Knight Tournament was only a month away, and Dennis would never take horse candy, or anything like it, ever again. He understood the bigger dangers ahead. Liver disease, tumors and cysts, a heart attack or stroke. Dennis was definitely more irritable. So far there wasn't any depression or suicidal tendencies, but he was on the lookout, and knew to be careful.

One more month, he kept telling himself, whenever he felt the candy doing its worst.

But then again, what if he couldn't stop?

Not because he was addicted, but because Orin might want to do something else after this. Dennis wouldn't want to refuse. This was the best bonding they'd ever had, and the closest they'd ever been. Even better than Scouts.

Orin was so determined to win this first challenge, what if he never wanted to stop?

And looking at himself naked, Dennis had never been happier. He looked better than he did at his peak, before Orin was born.

Maybe it wouldn't be so bad, for a little while longer.

Two years until Orin was a legal adult, and no longer eligible for the famili app adventures. A shaky hand wouldn't matter — Orin could be the marksman, and Dennis the leader.

"Better luck next time, Dad."

Dennis hadn't even finished squeezing off his final shot, but it sounded like Orin was waiting to say it.

"A quick pic before going?" Dennis felt hopeful, still a bit timid about taking and posting selfies after all their earlier conflict. But Orin said *Sure*, same as he had been, then posed with yet another well-practiced smile.

One more month.

"Remember," Dennis reminded Orin yet again, "not a word about this to your mother."

"Maybe we should stop on the way home and get a tattoo," Orin suggested. "Then you wouldn't have to keep telling me the same thing. I could just look down at my arm or whatever, whenever I needed the reminder. But then, maybe that's a bad idea, because we'd probably have to get me a second tattoo so I could remember not to tell Mom about the first one."

"I'm not trying to nag you, but your mother can be a little uptight. That's part of the reason we split up."

Orin looked at his father, long and hard, as if at war with himself, wondering if he should call Dennis out on his bullshit. Because of course he remembered that as uptight as his mother might have been, or even still was, that wasn't the reason his father came home stumbling drunk.

"Why don't we get lunch?" Dennis suggested. "Whatever you want."

"Great. There's this Thai place that's supposedly great. It's sorta by your place."

"Oh?" Dennis raised his eyebrows. "Where did you hear about it?"

"It's one of Ryan's favorites," he admitted with a shrug.

"How about Italian?"

"Why would you say we can eat wherever I want, then suggest something different?"

"I didn't expect you to pick Thai. Since when do you even *like* Thai?"

"Since there's a big tournament that you insisted we compete in, and now it's a month away and we should be watching what we eat."

"And Thai is that much healthier than Italian? You can order whatever you want."

"Do they have pad pak bung fai daeng?"

"I don't understand any of those words."

"It means stir-fried morning glory. It has spinach and stuff. Super healthy, and if you get it cooked without oyster sauce, it's low in sodium."

"How do you even know that?" Dennis asked, a moment before he realized the answer.

"I told you, it's one of Ryan's favorites."

"In this neighborhood?"

"He likes the trashy places."

"How about Podium?"

"What's that?" Orin asked.

"It's a steakhouse, and fancy."

"Fancy is expensive. I thought you were watching your money."

"You said you wanted to eat healthier, right? Something to make you stronger for the tournament — I'm not sure that you can do better than protein and vegetables."

"Agreed. Thai food is great for that."

"You might be the only non-vegetarian in the world, willing to turn down a steak dinner at—"

"Fine, dad. Let's eat at Podium, or wherever you want to. Sounds great."

Dennis was already annoyed that Orin of all people was nagging him to be a healthy eater, but then his son started agitating him even more.

"I'm really tired, and I'd like to get to sleep a little earlier. Would you mind answering all of our comments when we get home?"

Then he tucked some hair behind his ear in his annoying, arrogant way. It was getting even longer, and more tempting in moments like this. Dennis really wanted to rip it out of his head.

They drove home mostly in silence. Orin was listening to something on his juke, and Dennis was mindlessly swiping around the famili app.

He hadn't told Orin what he'd done, knowing that his son would probably scold him, but he had created an artificial family so he could log in to the app and check out what team Wilder was doing, undetected.

It wasn't just that Dennis didn't want the app to think he was a stalker. Dennis also wanted the option of leaving negative comments with the freedom of anonymity.

So far, Wilder had ignored everything that Dennis said, just like a jerk.

But he had finally taken the bait, responding to a string of disparaging comments, started by @suuuuuuuperdad (Dennis), fueled by @mrfamily (also Dennis), and rounded up, mostly at the end, by @doodad2000 (definitely the most Dennis of all).

His last comment read, *Nothing special, buying your way to the top.*

And Thomas responded, *Why don't you put up or shut up? At least I joined the Tournament. Pretty easy to throw rocks from the sidelines.*

"Check it out, Wilder's all in a huff." Laughing, he tried to hand Orin the phone.

Orin begrudgingly took it, then cast disinterested eyes at the screen before looking up at his father. "So?"

"So, look how rattled he is."

"He doesn't seem rattled to me. @doodad2000 seems like an asshole."

"The guy's not wrong. Team Wilder does buy their way to the top, we've always agreed about that, haven't we?"

"Sure, Dad."

"And that's why we're going to beat him!" Dennis felt genuinely excited, at the edge of the tournament, and as diligently trained as they were. Why was it so hard to get Orin equally excited? "Come on, son, give me a *Go Team Hoke!*"

"Go Team Hoke," Orin echoed, without any joy in his voice.

Chapter Fifteen

IT WAS two weeks before the big game and, as Dennis kept reminding himself, *Go time.*

Surprisingly, even Susan was on his side. Seeing Orin as happy as he obviously was in all those pictures must have really had an impact. She even agreed to let Dennis pick him up in the middle of the week for some extra practice. He felt bad that they were going to the shooting range, but it wasn't like he had any say about what challenges the Millennial Knight Tournament might offer, and Team Hoke needed to be prepared for everything.

It was such a pedestrian thing to do, picking up his son from school, but it had been years since he'd done anything like it, and Dennis was … *excited* seemed like a big word for what he was feeling, but it was nostalgic for sure, and maybe something more.

His car stopped in front of the steel and glass monument to adolescent socialization. Leaned back in his seat, and waited for Ryan to come out.

He whipped out his phone, swiped to the famili app — the thing was like a new best friend — and, of course,

@hawtestmom had messaged him four times. One would be naughty for sure; she hadn't dropped below twenty-five percent delivery rate in less than a week. The app gave him a pie chart and everything. Those messages were tagged as *dirty*, which came in about half of his number of overall *sweet*. A ratio famili liked.

Explicit photos were unavailable on the junior devices, but adult-themed conversations were huge, and therefore encouraged among famili's single parent user base.

Dennis hit the jackpot immediately. An impressive shot of @hawtestmom, bending over with her naughty bits visible, her face still autoblurred.

He gave her a smiley and was about to add a pic of his own, when he caught sight of something that withered his libido like two grapes baking in the sun.

Orin, talking to Ryan. *Laughing.*

What the fuck?

He closed famili and slipped the phone into his pocket. He sat there watching his son, trying not to boil, despite the cranking heat, burning hotter and hotter.

They stopped laughing, but only so they could start laughing harder. It looked like overacting in a skit, the two of them doubled over and heaving. They kept on guffawing, until it suddenly stopped.

Orin saw Dennis watching, then looked like he walked right into a wall.

He shook his head at Ryan, marched over to the car, got inside, and slammed the door.

"What was that all about?" Dennis asked.

"What was all what about?"

"That. The vaudeville act."

"I thought I was supposed to get close to Team Wilder. Look for weaknesses. Exploit thy enemy. Those are your words, right, Dad?"

"Home," Dennis said to the car. Then to Orin, "I don't think I ever said 'thy.'"

"You've said it more than once."

"That looked like you guys were on your way to a sleepover."

"Make up your mind, Dad. Did you want me to get close or not? And if so, did you want me to suck at it? Aren't you always telling me to be the best I can be, and stomp on our enemies' faces, especially if they're soft and privileged like the Wilders?"

Dennis had said all of that, but he'd been kidding, or at least had made it sound a lot more lighthearted than Orin's ugly parody.

"If it's working, great. I'm sorry. So, what do we know?"

Orin shrugged. "There really isn't anything *to* know."

"You two have been buddy-buddy for a while, and it looked like you were ready to share a yearbook photo, or maybe a milkshake, so you must have found something by now."

"Share a yearbook photo? Did that used to be a thing?"

"So, nothing?" Dennis pressed.

"They're really good."

"That's amazing, Orin. It's good we caught this early. You could have a career in corporate espionage."

"I never wanted to spy on my friends, or pretend to make friends to spy on."

"You said you wanted to win."

"I'm pretty sure you said that for me. And if I said it, this definitely isn't what I meant."

"But you're having a good time."

"What do you want me to say, Dad? I guess I'm having as good a time as I can, given the circumstances."

"What's that supposed to mean?"

"I don't know why you have a broom handle up your pucker about Ryan and his dad. They've always been nice to us. Ryan wants me to make a video game with him. He's really good at coding."

"You hate Ryan!"

"I've never hated Ryan. I just knew you didn't want me to be friends with him, and that you didn't like his father."

"You said Phoebe liked him."

"She did like him, but so what?"

"So … isn't that the point? Isn't that one of the reasons we started this? Are you trying to make me feel old, and like I can't remember things right?" Dennis laughed, making sure that Orin knew he wasn't mad.

"I'm just saying that you never gave them a chance, and they've always been nice."

"They can afford to be nice! They have tons of money, and connections. You know how much easier it is to be nice when you're not worried about owing more than a hundred credits on your phone bill? That doesn't mean they see us as equals. It doesn't matter how nice Thomas Wilder is to my face, that guy is always looking down his nose at me. That's what people like him do."

"Ryan's not like that."

"He'll get there."

"You don't know him."

"I know enough. And why are you defending him? If we lose to them, it'll be all your fault."

Orin didn't answer, falling into a long stretch of what felt like performative quiet.

There was something different in his silence. It wasn't sulky or sour. Nothing sullen about it. It was a patient tranquility, as though Orin had all the time in the world.

A silence that bristled with danger, pregnant from with-held satisfaction.

Torment awaiting reply.

He'd really grown up. Still his son, but now less boy than man.

Dennis felt a deep, almost overwhelming sense of pride.

Maybe he had pushed Orin into this, but he had made him a stronger, more capable young man. After all he'd suffered through, and managed to put behind him, Dennis was finally the kind of father he had always wanted to be.

Chapter Sixteen

THE TOURNAMENT WAS one week away.

In so many ways it felt like Dennis had been waiting his entire life for this. It had been a struggle, with all the baggage between him and Susan. Yes, he fell, collapsed, failed as a husband and a father. But as hard as it was to bar himself from the bottle, show up every day at work without fail, tend to every animal as if it were his own, no matter what else he might have been going through, and eventually clawing his way back into Orin's good graces, he had done it. Found the line between friend and parent, then rode it so admirably.

He let Orin pick all of their training, and become the man that had made his father so proud. It was almost overwhelming. As Orin sat next to him on the couch, looking at the new, just-released map of the tournament route, Dennis felt emotional, almost like crying.

His phone dinged with another comment, but Dennis ignored it.

This deserved his full attention, and he didn't want Orin to think he was distracted, even if he was only checking his phone to see the famili app. To check on how they were doing, and maybe see if @hawtestmom had sent another picture of ice melting on her nipple.

Orin had been staring at the map for minutes without blinking. His studious gaze was all over it, pinching in and zooming out, schooling himself on the countless hints hidden like secrets sprinkled throughout the route, challenges scattered, abundant items to find and benefit from.

He finally looked up. "It's different than we thought."

We. Dennis wanted to hug him.

Instead he nodded. "Yeah, but maybe that's okay. Everyone else was probably expecting a flatter area, too. But so what? Who cares if it's hill country. We trained for everything. Let the Wilders worry ... Sorry," Dennis corrected himself. "Let everyone worry. We'll be fine."

His phone dinged again, but he continued to ignore it.

The tournament was in the hill country about two hours outside of town.

Their objective was to reach a small lake house on the shore. Or more specifically, the flag inside it. Last team holding the flag won the tournament, and could claim the title of that year's Millennial Knight. Alliances weren't allowed, with every team sighted on number one.

"Let's go work out," Orin suggested.

"I told you, we can't."

"No, you said you didn't want to."

"I said that I wanted to follow best practices. There are banners all over famili suggesting that competitors take it easy the week before the tournament. We've gone on two walks already, and we did yoga. We're in peak shape. Wouldn't you rather play *HardCorps*?"

His phone buzzed.

"You can get it," Orin said, with the slightest bit irritation creeping into his voice, though maybe Dennis was being oversensitive.

He shouldn't have grabbed it, but he did.

The comments were coming in batches. Fifty-three new ones from the last three dings alone.

Dennis looked up from his phone. "Why don't we take a selfie in our war room?"

"Or we could focus on actually coming up with a battle plan. You know, for the tournament we're wanting to win."

"We are going to win," Dennis grinned. "And you know why? Because winning over our fanbase is half the battle, and we've been doing the hell out of that. Come on."

He positioned himself behind Orin, held the phone out for the photo.

Orin stayed put, but refused to smile.

"Oh, that's great," Dennis said. "We should have our game faces on."

He changed his expression to match Orin's, shot the photo, then took another and another after that, Orin looking irritated more than serious in each of them.

"Fiercer. More intense," Dennis suggested. "Like this."

He twisted his face into a parody of an action hero, ready to storm the gates. Then he looked at Orin, disappointed. "You're not even trying."

"I don't like fake smiling, Dad. We've talked about it."

They had, and Dennis still had plenty to say, but he would have to swallow it, same as he had been. Teenagers were moody, his included. Even a great dad couldn't change biology. Focus on the positives, and of those there were plenty.

Dennis had been training his ass off, and Orin had been training even harder.

And there was that pride again, swelling his chest, and

catching in his throat.

He'd never seen his son work harder for anything, or want something so bad.

Orin would stop at nothing to get what he wanted, and Dennis had given him that drive. Even Susan admitted to being impressed. He jogged after school every day now, and was always practicing, though she didn't know he was throwing knives. Or need to. Susan knew about his climbing trees, and was finally warmed enough to archery that she'd taken him to a local range, even gave him seven credits to spend an evening there once his homework was all done.

She was even helping, in her way. Supporting Orin with grilled meat and salads, making his protein shakes in the morning and before bed, even paying for them without bitching about it.

No wonder Orin was so grouchy, Dennis felt a little moody himself, and he wasn't nearly as strict with his diet. But everything was temporary. This would all be over soon.

The tournament was in a week, and a better life was waiting on the other side.

The one he and his son had earned together.

They needed a well-deserved break, and that should have been obvious to them both.

"Why don't we treat ourselves to some pizza?" Dennis suggested.

"No thanks."

"I know, I know, you want one of your shakes. But we should take a break, and you deserve to eat some pizza. Remember how much you used to love pizza?"

"I still love pizza, and of course I remember, it hasn't been that long since I've had it. But I haven't eaten anything like that in over a month."

"Exactly, you deserve—"

"You're not listening to me. It's not a matter whether I deserve it or not, I don't want it."

"But it's pizza …"

"And I don't want pizza tonight. At all. And besides, I told you I was going to chat with @adorkable tonight."

"Oh yeah … who is he again?"

The name sounded familiar. Someone Orin had met on LiveLyfe.

"He's done a lot of hiking in the area. I met him online while I was looking for people who have spent a lot of time on the trails up there."

Made sense, and Orin had told him, now that Dennis remembered it.

Gamers were prohibited from visiting the contest site after the location's announcement, but Orin had wanted to know all he could, and had apparently managed to track down someone who could tell him whatever he needed to know.

@adorkable was going to make that happen.

"Hey, will you look at this?" Dennis said, trying to show him a comment. "Don't you think that seems a bit stalker-ish?"

Orin had no interest, wouldn't even glance up to see what his father was talking about.

"I'm serious. You should take a look."

But Orin still wasn't looking, and Dennis wondered how hard he should push it. The girl did seem like a stalker, leaving over twenty comments today alone. And while she wasn't in any way unattractive, she wasn't exactly Phoebe. Her username was @ShyErin.

And definitely not the type of girl that Ryan Wilder would ever be interested in.

"Fine then, don't look. But you should at least hear this." Dennis threw his voice into the highest pitch he could manage, then did an awful impersonation of what he imagined a teenage girl must sound like. "You're so hot — I've watched all of your videos twice. I've been following you and your dad's journey since the beginning. I know it sounds silly, but I feel like I actually know you. Like we'd get along so good. I can't wait to see you at the finish line! I'll start watching all of your videos again until then!"

"That's great, Dad."

"Seriously, you don't think that's a little creepy? Feels like she knows you, feels like you'd get along so good?"

Orin shrugged.

"What are you going to say to her?"

But Orin didn't answer. "Half the prize money is mine, right?"

"Well, yeah. Of course."

"And you promised I could have it right away.

That was out of the blue, and more than a little rude. Dennis said he'd never drink again, and he hadn't touched a drop. He said he'd be a better father to Orin, and he had been. Better than his own had ever been. Dennis always kept his promises.

"Of course half the money is yours. Isn't that what we agreed, and what I said?"

"You say a lot of things."

"What's *that* supposed to mean?" Dennis asked.

Orin's phone started ringing before he could answer.

He snatched it from the table like it might explode if he didn't.

"Hello?" Orin said, already on his way out the sliding glass door to take the call on Dennis's crappy little balcony.

He had been doing that a lot.

Dennis hoped he was talking to Phoebe, because then he wouldn't take Orin's desire for privacy so personally. At sixteen years old, and talking to a girl like that, Dennis would've wanted a little freedom from disturbance, too. He tried interrupting once before, but Orin wasn't having it. Dennis wasn't even trying to eavesdrop, or listen in at all. He just wanted to be around his son while he was talking, and if he happened to pick up a stray clue, then all the better for him.

"Did you need something?" Orin had asked him, before he stopped speaking to whomever was on the other end, staring at his father until he finally went away.

After that, Orin started taking all of his calls on the balcony.

That was fine, at least Dennis could go ahead and order their pizza. Orin didn't have to be a Puritan or a martyr. No need to be a workhorse right now. Not tonight.

The time was finally here. This was their last chance to have even a small break before the grueling tournament next weekend. Orin only thought that pizza sounded like a bad idea. Once he smelled a fresh meat-lover's sitting in an open box, he would forget all about his unnecessary need to punish himself with spinach and green beans, or whatever it was Orin thought he wanted to eat instead of pizza during their rare time together.

So Dennis opened the pizza app, ordered Orin's favorite, included payment and tip, then swiped over to his favorite friend in the famili app.

The delivery would arrive shortly, so while Orin was outside talking to his secret girlfriend, Dennis would talk to @hawtestmom. She was now apparently determined to be his number one fan. Enough to finally show him her face.

The woman's face was as hot as her body. And she played a good game. More dirty DMs, while easing up on the naughty pictures. She was down to a pair, one in the morning and another before bed, always appropriately themed. She promised to keep sending two per day.

Dennis already knew what he was going to do if — *when* — he was one of this year's two Millennial Knights. Celebrate with Orin, then take a one-week vacation from the clinic, asking @hawtestmom which she prefers, between Cabo and Cozumel.

Have you ever vacationed in Mexico? he DM'd her.

A knock on his door. The pizza was here.

Dennis set down his phone, went to the door, grabbed the box from a startled teenager's hand, leaving her blinking in surprise and falling into the hallway as Dennis said, "Sorry," then slipped back inside and shut the door.

With the bill and tip paid for, apparently Dennis was too busy for simple human decency.

He wanted to see what @hawtestmom had written back, now that he'd put it all out there, and Dennis was also dying to get Orin back into the apartment. An open box and rolling waves of aroma might just do the trick.

He went to the balcony, cursing the sliding glass door for sticking in the frame like it always did, opened it wide, then walked away without saying a thing, giving Orin time, just in case he needed a minute or two.

"I gotta go," he said to the phone.

Then Orin came inside, closed the door behind him, and spoke to Dennis like there wasn't a piping hot pizza with all of his favorite toppings sitting right there on the table.

"I'm going for a walk."

"You don't want any pizza?"

"I told you I didn't want pizza before you ordered it."

"Right, but you hadn't smelled it yet."

Orin shook his head, eyes impatient.

"What are you going to eat?"

Orin shrugged.

"You have to eat something."

"I'm not hungry."

"I'll go with you. On your walk," Dennis offered.

"No thanks. I'm not up for company right now."

There was nothing else that Dennis could say. He simply sighed as Orin walked out the door.

Then he sighed again, going to sit alone and eat some meat lover's all by himself.

Dennis supposed it made sense. When you got in a fight with your girlfriend, you definitely wanted space. His call had ended abruptly. He'd probably been stuck in one of those teenage fights, born out of hormones from nowhere, fueled by unnecessary but unfortunately unavoidable teenage hysteria.

At least the pizza was good, and @hawtestmom loved Mexico. Tequila was her favorite liquor to get drunk on. It made her feel dirty faster, and @hawtestmom slurred so terribly, she could barely ever manage to even slur the word *No*, or so she told him.

Another alert.

Dennis swiped to see it.

And things really did keep getting better and better.

Their famili social score was a full fifty percent higher than Team Wilder's.

There was little doubt they were going to win.

And once the pressure of the contest was behind them, Orin would be happy. And relaxed.

Dennis would get custody, and this time Susan wouldn't fight him.

It was his turn, and at Orin's age now, Dennis was better equipped for the job.

Soon, it would be the two of them, all the time.

And they would be an even better team than they already were.

Chapter Seventeen

THE TOURNAMENT WAS TOMORROW.

But Dennis couldn't sleep. His insomnia had been getting worse. A steady creep since two weeks after he started taking the horse candy.

No big deal at first, he didn't even realize it was happening. Or that there was a pattern.

One night having a hard time followed another.

Then a night where he could barely sleep at all, finally crashing around five in the morning, giving him around a half hour before he had to wake up for his early shift at Furry Friends.

But tonight was the worst it had been, and during what was probably the most important night's sleep of his life.

The anxiety made it worse.

Like not being able to get hard because you couldn't get hard.

Dennis thought he might die awake.

He turned over. Flirted with the idea of checking his phone, but the light would only make things worse.

Not that it mattered.

He wasn't going to sleep.

Not tonight.

Though if he checked his phone, Dennis might see another message from @hawtestmom. She had already sent her pic for the night.

But there was nothing after that, and now Dennis knew it for sure. Same as every other one of the times he checked.

He really needed to sleep.

Dennis tried naming all fifty states, but lost count and ran out of ones he knew off the top of his head around thirty-something.

He started thinking about Cabo, because @hawtestmom went there for spring break when she was twenty, and thought it sounded like a great place to relive some of her wilder days.

He thought about a week in Mexico and that made him think of Susan and what an uptight bitch she had always been, and still was.

Unfortunately, she blew it, and now Dennis was going to be someone else's world.

Because ...

Dennis caught himself, almost drifting off.

But that was good, he could fall asleep thinking of @hawtestmom,

and how tomorrow he'd finally know her name,

and how things were so great with Orin and about to be better than ever,

and how Susan was going to be so sorry that she left him,

and how he couldn't wait to move to a bigger place, once he had all that tournament money,

and ...

Chapter Eighteen

THE TOURNAMENT WAS FINALLY HERE.

Dennis and Orin were at Meadow Crest, the sweeping lawns at the base of a beautiful, rolling hill. Starting spot for the Millennial Knight Tournament, and ground zero for a much better life.

Dennis had been waiting for this. Same for his son. He was thick with pride, looking at Orin and how obviously ready he was to win.

Fathers and sons were everywhere.

Mothers and daughters, mothers and sons, fathers and daughters.

Combinations Dennis couldn't figure out, and didn't need to.

And the place was a riot of color. Clusters of balloons that were thicker than the clouds. A sea of people, with most of them smiling. Electricity in the air, charged with the expectations inherent in a truly life-changing event, even for the losers.

Even though it would all be torn down once the tournament was over, the staging looked permanent. The food court could have had been comprised of simple plywood stalls. Instead they had faux architecture to match the region of cuisine. An adobe shack for Mexican, a thatched hut for Chinese, a tiny café for Italian. It was all impressive, and Dennis couldn't help think about all the sultry waitresses as Kitty Kat Bubbles.

The lodge loomed ahead. A battalion of TVs were set up for spectators to watch the contest. Drones would capture hundreds of perspectives, and each contestant would be wearing overlay goggles with ear plants. A tiny camera recording every second. The online audience, which was apparently massive — much larger than Dennis had realized — could stream any contestant's video, past or present, and follow commentary centered on their favorite team or team member.

The banners were big enough to welcome the president, celebrating Millennial Knight hopefuls such as Dennis and Orin, friends and family, and everyone watching at home. Sponsors, including Nostalgia Inc, the makers of famili, apparently the assholes responsible for all the ads Dennis always saw in his feed. They weren't obnoxious like most app environments, or going online in general, but were still oddly effective.

Dennis didn't know why, but he ended up looking into the famili ads more than any other ads he'd ever regularly seen, and feeling almost overwhelmingly pleased with his purchase.

"You got all that?" Dennis asked, nodding at Orin's gear.

"Of course."

The kid was confident. Ready. Maybe even more so than Dennis.

Of course he was. Dennis had barely slept.

But he'd taken some extra horse candy, and was feeling

as prepared as could be expected. Not to mention opti-
mistic. His time had been coming, and this was finally it.
Dennis had already done more with Orin in sixteen years
than his father had done with him throughout his entire
life. And that included all the years that Susan had forced
them apart.

This was the payoff for three months and a lifetime of
bonding.

They approached the lodge, wading through a mob of
people, including a flock of girls heading straight for Orin,
squealing louder by the step.

"You're Orin Hoke! I'm ShyErin," yelled the loudest,
oldest, boobiest one. She was twenty or so and didn't seem
all that shy in person. The youngest of the seven standing
around his son was perhaps eleven or twelve.

Orin took the attention like a man. He nodded, smiled,
and thanked them. But he didn't let it go to his head, or
allow his gaze to stray from their target for more than a
couple of moments.

But ShyErin gathered her gaggle and got them to
scamper back in front of him.

"We made you this!" She thrust a T-shirt into his
hands.

Orin unfolded it: *yOrin our thoughts!*

"Get it?" asked the youngest girl.

"Thanks," he smiled, then neatly folded the shirt and
tucked it into his backpack.

"Well that was cool," Dennis said, several steps away
from the flock.

Before he could answer, @hawtestmom appeared out
of nowhere, a few feet in front of him.

Their eyes locked. He opened his mouth to say something, but then closed it as she marched across the twenty
feet of lawn between them.

She didn't stop in front of him, practically crashing into Dennis as her mouth mashed against his, her tongue swimming upstream between his lips. He licked her back and she nipped at his bottom lip, playfully tugging it between her teeth before letting it go between her warm, wet lips.

She pulled away and left him panting. Then she looked around, smiling at all the people who had caught it on video.

"That oughta get us some smileys," she whispered, then winked. "I'll be waiting for you in the victory circle."

Us, she said.

Dennis was stunned, still hadn't moved even though @hawtestmom was now walking away.

He watched her ass get smaller, then turned back to Orin, expecting to see his son's admiring eyes. But Orin wasn't where Dennis expected, and before he could figure out what was happening, an open palm slapped him hard across the face.

He had to catch his breath, holding his burning cheek.

What the fuck was that?

He blinked.

Susan. Standing in front of Orin, a few feet to the side.

"What the hell was that for?" Dennis asked.

"Nothing better happen to our son in this stupid contest."

Dennis had no idea what she was so puckered about. Orin was doing just fine, and obviously so was he, though maybe that was the problem.

He was still slightly drunk from arousal. Surprisingly, Susan hadn't upset it. If anything, he felt turned-on knowing what she'd seen, and would soon be missing out on.

The bell rang. Last call to get into the lodge.

"We gotta go," Dennis told Orin.

"I've been ready."

Susan wished them luck, genuinely to their son, but begrudgingly to Dennis.

Moments later, Team Hoke was standing in the lodge along with everyone else.

Then contestants were led out the other side, and onto a dead and ugly lawn.

Even though it had gone from storybook facades to a withered field scattered with ramshackle plywood buildings, scavenged parts, and old Quonset huts, the layout still felt staged.

"Hey there, Team Hoke," Thomas said as the Wilders were walking by. "Good luck with the tournament today!"

"Don't need it," Dennis said.

He looked over to Orin, grinning, but Orin wasn't looking back at him.

Instead, he and Ryan were trading a glance.

Suspicion like a spear, sinking into his flesh.

Dennis told himself to ignore it.

But that wasn't easy. A second after Dennis gave himself the directive, he thought about how Orin and Ryan had been talking at school, and yet Orin hadn't come home with a single piece of actionable intel about Team Wilder's plans.

Here it was, game day, and Dennis felt suddenly naked without them.

Orin was a good kid, but maybe too naive.

What if he'd gone into the lion's den, only to discover Ryan was actually a serpent?

He could have been the one to trick Orin, convince him they were friends, because he wanted to unpack what Team Hoke was doing, then take advantage of his so-called friend.

Orin told him that Ryan wanted to make computer games. So he probably knew how to bug Orin's phone. Easy enough to accomplish if they were friends. Ryan could have cloned it, or whatever hackers did to listen in on an unsuspecting person's conversations.

What if Team Wilder knew everything? Knew what they were best at, what they struggled with, what their strategies for each portion of the contest were.

What if Orin had gift wrapped the Wilders' victory without even knowing it?

Dennis was an idiot.

He should have thought of this. Taken the proper precautions.

He was about to ask a leading question about Ryan, but Orin said, "Who was that woman who kissed you? That was weird, right?"

"Yeah, totally weird."

Dennis wasn't about to disagree. Not before the tournament started. He hadn't done anything wrong, but he didn't want to have any back and forth about it now. Orin didn't need to know about his chats with @hawtestmom, or the pictures, or their plans to go south of the border.

"Did you know her?" Orin pressed.

"I guess she's just a super fan."

"Is that @hawtestmom?"

"You know about @hawtestmom?"

"Of course I know about @hawtestmom. She comments on everything you post. And has like a million mouthy friends. You're really telling me she's never DM'd you?"

"Yeah, of course. A couple of times."

The intercom crackled, coming alive with a voice that sounded like it belonged by a campfire. "Hello everyone ..."

The crowd turned as one toward the handsomely deco-rated stage, and the dapper man standing in its center. His suit looked pressed from the darkness itself, yet still it shined in the sun, black and soft and glimmering. It fit him like a drawing. Sharply parted hair, silky and dark, sharply cut his profile into thirds, with one side handsome, and the other slightly more than twice as much. His teeth gleamed like they wanted to sell something, and when the man smiled, it held the kind of promise broken only by an act of God.

"I'm Mr. Jones, your host. And I'd like to welcome you to the Millennial Knight Tournament."

Mr. Jones waited for the applause to die, then he continued.

"I'm from Nostalgia Inc, a proud sponsor of this event." He chuckled. "*The* proud sponsor of this event. We're in the business of making memories. And every one of you here today will remember parts of this tournament for the rest of your life."

Another round of applause. Jones let it roll, then settle.

"If you are here now, we can assume that you've done your training. That you're well-rested. And that you are ready to compete for the title of Millennial Knight." Then, slightly louder, "Is that right?"

More applause.

"And are you ready to make memories?"

The applause hadn't stopped from the last time, and more people were joining.

"These glasses will help you to make those memories. But they must stay on the entire time. Remove them and you will be disqualified. Please, if you'll don your overlays." He waited several beats, smiled wide again, then said, "Now, behind me …"

Mr. Jones turned and swept a wide arcing hand, a ringmaster presenting his circus.

"Hopefuls for the title of Millennial Knight must survive the ghost town, brave the horrors of the hillside forest, and find the two keys unlocking the secrets of an ancient temple in the middle of Lake Despondent."

"If you haven't studied your maps, it's too late now. If you have, then may the best team win! Get ready to go in five …"

Dennis looked through his overlay, and the effect was amazing. The prop masters had already done an impressive job of setting the stage. But now it didn't look like the backdrop for what might become an Old West ghost town. It *was* an Old West ghost town.

"Four … three …"

The first round of elimination, designed to whittle the teams to a reasonable number. A combination of scavenger hunt and laser tag.

The effect was incredible. Despite the contestants all looking like cowboys to each other, they felt that way, too. Dennis patted his chest and felt the zippered pockets. He was still in his special body suit, the one he'd practiced on in the dark, drawing items from its many depths, so he could do it by feel without looking. Orin's suggestion, and another great one at that. Their laser pistols had turned into Colt 45s with laser sights on them, and they'd never run out of ammo.

"Two … you have sixty seconds, before you can shoot in … ONE!"

A shot rang out, disqualifying someone.

Everyone else *ran*.

Chapter Nineteen

THERE WERE TOO many contestants in the tournament for everyone to start in the same section, so they were herded into varying groups, with a hundred players — fifty pairings — per mass.

"Follow me," Dennis said, pointing at the virtual yellow line leading them to an alley between a saloon and a milliner's. If he took his goggles off, the illusion would disappear, but right now it was startling, slightly disorienting even.

He wanted to reach out and touch the glass in front of the saloon, run his finger along the fine layer of dust on the swinging wooden doors, kicked up from the unpaved Main Street, running down the center of an abandoned mining town called Lowmire Flats, according to the weathered sign. Dennis felt compelled to grab one of the Victorian hats from the milliner's window display, just to feel the velvet in his hands.

They ducked into the alleyway. Orin looked intense, probably studying the readout, same as Dennis. The display would tell them their mission objective. To find a chest full of loot, stolen by the Jonas Gang, from the good people who happened to be taking the 8:51 to Laredo from Lowmire, or so said the Wanted Poster plastered to the alley wall.

"We'll have to search the town and avoid getting killed by any of the other teams. Every one of them will be looking."

"Right," Orin agreed. "That's why they came here."

"So we need to—"

Dennis didn't finish before a bullet whizzed by him and thunked into the wood. He couldn't even take a second to be impressed. He dashed out of the alley, then turned and fired blindly.

Fortunately, Orin was sharper. He spun around, pulled his trigger three times, and turned the adolescent kid into a skeleton in chaps and spurs.

"Dammit!" yelled the skeleton kid, trudging off in the other direction.

Orin turned to Dennis, grinning wide, obviously proud and—

He flinched, seemed to catch something with a sixth sense, looked up to the roof, and let loose another trio of shots. Then they listened to more muttering and swearing as the second player went down.

"Look out!" Dennis yelled, instead of taking the shot for himself.

And the dreaded voice yelled in his ear: *What kind of a pussy are you?*

But again, Orin was ready. He aimed and shot, three seemed to be his number, then another cowboy — looking like kin to the kid on the roof — got three slugs in the back before turning into a skeleton.

"Three down, ninety-seven to go," Orin said, still grinning.

"Stay behind me." Dennis stepped ahead of his son, after giving him a direction he didn't need to follow, and probably shouldn't if they expected to stay alive. Still, it felt like the right thing to say as they made their way down Main Street, deeper into the tiny town, clearing and searching buildings, just like an ex-Green Beret at the shooting range taught them, seamlessly working as a team.

Another five players down. A tough-looking girl and her mother (that Orin looked disappointed to send home), what looked like a bratty-looking ten-year-old and his even brattier dad, and a stray cowboy, with long silver streaks in his beard that may or may not have been a product of the goggles. Dennis managed to down that last one.

The only thing that could have made this adventure any better was running into Team Wilder. Dennis was ready to eliminate their asses the second they could.

Orin was still on fire, another four players down in the next two minutes, thanks to reflexes that were practically smoking.

All four contestants saw him first, but Orin was always the faster draw.

There were a long several moments where they both felt watched. Dennis asked about it, but Orin hushed him.

Something was watching. But the thing wasn't human.

They finally saw it when they entered the Lowmire Sheriff's Office and saw what the map hadn't told them.

The place was thick with zombies, or at least all four of the cells were. Though the zombie sheriff wasn't locked up in one of them, still drooling like all the rest.

"Are those players who have been killed?" Dennis asked.

"No, Dad. They're zombies."

"That's what I was thinking … but how do you know?"

"Because we turn into skeletons when we're shot, not zombies. Those are obviously part of the game."

"So we're going to have to shoot them in the head, right? Because they're zombies."

The sheriff lurched toward Dennis.

He screamed, falling back, wrestling with his gun, trying to aim it.

But he couldn't get it steady in time, and the zombie sheriff was almost on him.

Another three shots from Orin — all in the head — and the zombie went down.

"I'm sure you lose points if it touches you," Orin said, as if his father didn't know.

And now Dennis felt embarrassed, losing his shit in front of his son.

But Orin laughed, kind rather than mocking, then Dennis started laughing too.

And he felt warm inside, because this was exactly what he had wanted the game to do for them from the very beginning, give them experiences that they could talk — and laugh — about for years.

Nostalgia Inc was perfectly named. They really did put experience above everything else.

"Come on, let's get going." Orin stepped over the sheriff's corpse and out onto the street as the zombies moaned and groaned and clawed at their bars.

Dennis followed, turning on the other side of the threshold to see the zombie sheriff standing, his head still rotting, but back to the way it had looked before they explored the dusty precinct, as though Orin hadn't filled him with bullets.

As much fun as Dennis was having, he wanted to feel like a contributor more than he was. But the deeper they went into Lowmire, the less valuable he felt. Orin had remarkable reflexes, an assassin's aim, and what seemed to be a sixth sense for anticipating enemies — or flat out knowing when one was nearby. Dennis had envisioned himself as the leader, directing Orin through the game, and having the consistent gratification of seeing his son looking up to him with mounting respect.

But instead, it felt more like he was riding on Orin's coattails.

So what. Even so, he should still feel proud. Orin had come into his own as a person, and that was a result of training he would have never undertaken without his father's inspiration. He was loving every minute, and that wouldn't be possible without training from instructors like Goliath, and relentless encouragement from his dad.

They entered a total of seven separate residences, but only had to deal with another three opponents. And the Wilders were still nowhere in sight.

They found the chest full of loot in the seventh home, a present from the Jonas Gang.

They slowly approached it, expecting some sort of trick, the two of them creeping toward the chest, faintly glowing blue.

But there was no gold inside it. No jewelry, bearer bonds, or anything else.

Only the true treasure, a secret code that would unlock the next part of their game. The second Dennis touched the chest, he code appeared on the visual display, popping up in his peripheral vision.

It was surreal. The virtual overlay made Dennis see a room that wasn't there, filled with old-fashioned furniture.

He couldn't take off his goggles just because he was curious. Orin would kill him twice. But he lifted them a little, just enough to get a peek under the rim, and long enough to see that the gorgeous antiques were really nothing more than mountains and molehills of modern junk, probably scavenged from thrift stores at best and junkyards more likely.

Everything was roughly the same size and shape, but the disconnect was startling. Enough to give Dennis an ache in his head to match the one in his stomach.

He lowered his goggles, and the disconnect instantly faded.

The world felt immediately better.

"You have the code?" Orin asked.

Dennis nodded.

"Then let's get out of here."

Orin headed toward the door, but halfway there he saw a flicker of motion through one of the windows and fell into a crouch, looking back to make sure his father was doing the same.

Dennis did, but it was a full moment later, and long enough to embarrass him.

He needed to do better. Not just in front of Orin; everyone was watching via the many cameras set up everywhere.

Especially @hawtestmom.

Dennis smiled, suddenly self-conscious.

Focus, he told himself.

"I think someone's out there." Orin grabbed a nearby vase off of an end table, then held it over his head so it was visible in the window.

A red dot appeared on the vase.

Orin turned to his father. "There's definitely someone out there. I think he's on the roof."

He tapped on his right temple twice, as if thinking. An odd gesture, striking Dennis almost like a tic.

"I'm not sure what you want me to do."

"Don't worry about it," Orin said.

"We'll have to sneak out back. We can't let ourselves get trapped." But then Dennis caught movement through a window of zombies waiting in that direction. He wasn't sure how many, but more than a couple.

"Or we could just walk out of here with guns blazing," Orin suggested.

Another two taps on his temple and Dennis felt bad, realizing what he was seeing. The pressure of the game — the pressure of *winning* — finally getting to Orin. He was struggling to handle it, and the tic was proof.

"We can't just walk out there, Orin. We'll be dead."

Dennis hated the weakness in his voice, but what choice did they have?

He started to worry if maybe this was it, if maybe they wouldn't be able to escape.

It would be a tragedy, losing it so close to the end, or at least the end of the beginning.

They already found the chest, and had their secret code. Now all they needed to do was make it to the edge of town, then run to the rendezvous point.

As long as they made it out of Lowmire, Team Hoke would automatically be qualified for the next part of the game, getting a free pass, permitting them to race uphill to the rope bridge and whatever waited for them next.

But they were sitting ducks if they stayed. Dead if they tried to escape.

"You have the best chance to make it, so I'll go first," Dennis offered, making his face brave, and throwing a quiver into his voice. "You shoot the guy out front while he's distracted. Let him take me out. You can still win this, even without your old man."

Orin rolled his eyes. "I'm going upstairs to see if I can get a better angle on him."

Dennis spun around toward a loud creak behind him.

Orin did the same, but he had his gun drawn by the time he finished his turn, and managed to pop off the right shots, eliminating the guy who had sneaked in from the back.

"I knew I was going to die in the first round," the skeleton sighed. "Well, good luck, guys."

Orin smiled at the skeleton, as though the kid hadn't just been trying to kill him. "Thanks."

Dennis peeked out the front window and saw another adolescent set of bones climbing down from the building across the street — the shooter that had been aiming at them.

Then he saw movement down the street as Wilder disappeared around the corner.

"I see Tom!" Dennis shouted, a moment before he realized.

No ...

He hadn't just been saved by Thomas Wilder, had he?

As much as Dennis hated to face it, that appeared to be the case. He was itching to run out after him, and shoot the asshole in his entitled back, but that would be the wrong thing to do.

They had their treasure. It would be idiotic to stick around hunting other players when the smartest possible move right now was reaching the far side of the Lowmire border.

"Someone got that shooter on the roof!" Dennis told Orin, no need to say who. "Let's move."

"Agreed."

He hadn't done enough in phase one, but that wasn't a giant surprise, seeing as shooting wasn't really his forte.

But now they would be moving into the next phase of the tournament.

Soon he would have another chance to prove himself as a team leader.

And even more importantly, his worth as a father.

Chapter Twenty

Dennis and Orin raced across the ghost town's virtual border.

Home free!

His heart pounded for all the right reasons.

"That was amazing," Dennis said.

"Yeah. Cool. Let's get to the trailhead."

Orin was a worker. Why stop and celebrate victory when you could keep on going and prove that your last win wasn't a fluke?

They were supposed to be jogging at most, no reason to get winded this early. They didn't know what would be facing them in the next phase. But Orin was moving fast, and Dennis wasn't about to show his age.

He caught up, trying to hide his panting, working his breath into a steady rhythm before he said, "How many teams remaining?"

A virtual readout appeared in front of him. The first round hit the contestants hard. They were down to twelve intact teams, plus four lone warriors who had been separated from either their parent or child.

Team Wilder was among the survivors.

And according to the readout, they were making their way up the mountain already.

Dammit!

"We need to get going."

"We are going," Orin said, obviously running slower than he wanted to, and waiting for Dennis to catch up.

They must have already found their treasure, and were on their way out of Lowmire when they ran into the shooter on the roof. Now the Wilders were ahead of the Hokes.

Dennis wanted to catch them, more than anything. If he could just eliminate the Wilders, then surely the ultimate win would be theirs. Guys like that had been taking from Dennis his entire life. He couldn't allow it here, not here nor ever again.

If Dennis could take them out of the game, he would be eliminating the only thing standing between him, Orin, and the life they deserved. And didn't Dennis and Orin deserve the win, and the prize, more? This was just another trophy on a shelf sagging beneath the weight of so many others for the Wilders. But for Dennis and Orin this really meant something. Surely, they deserved it more.

"Almost there," Dennis panted.

Orin didn't even grunt in agreement. Stoic, like the good son he was.

The hike was a punishment. Dennis had death on his shoulders, his pack gaining pounds by the hour, and feeling like a cross on his shoulder.

Up the trail they went. Every minute or so, Dennis would pull out his phone and check to see how far Team Wilder was ahead of the Hokes, then mutter under his breath and walk faster.

The famili app wouldn't show him where they were

exactly, because it wanted to avoid ambushes, but the display showed him where everyone was on the overall scale. Fortunately for now, both teams were still in phase two.

A flash in the trees. Movement and the swishing of fabric.

"Did you see that?" Dennis asked.

"No. Keep walking."

They did, but Dennis was sure he saw something.

He had to ignore it. Keep walking. Orin was almost robotic, marching like a video game character, with the player mashing his thumb all the way forward.

They reached the rope bridge, and thankfully it was almost exactly like the one they had trained on. About sixty feet from one end to the other, about fifteen feet off the ground. And like the one Goliath instructed them to cross, there was a massive trampoline and a large foam mat to catch any of the contestants who fell and eliminated themselves from the game.

Another treasure awaited those who made it to the middle.

"I've got it," Orin said. "You stand guard until I get back. Then we'll go around."

"No!" Dennis felt guilty that Orin was carrying the load, but also hurt to hear his son giving him orders. He was great at the tournament, but still, Dennis was supposed to be the leader. Not the other way around.

"You're the best shot. You should stay down here and cover me while I get the treasure."

Orin shook his head. "I'll be faster, and that means less exposure. Me not going is stupid."

A slap in the face, but not one he could argue with. Of course Orin was right. It didn't make any sense, his going for the treasure. Dennis had passed the rope bridge and all the climbing tests, but only barely. He was the slowest in both, and by an embarrassing disparity.

But that was before the horse candy. And all the training. Dennis was stronger now than he was then. "You're right," he said, feeling defeated. "You should go."

Orin nodded, then climbed the tree and eased his way out onto the bridge. The first few steps were impressive, he danced like a monkey, and the rope was like a sidewalk beneath him.

But a quarter of the way across something swooped out of the trees — a harpy attacking his kid with its claws.

Dennis cried out, then slapped a hand over his mouth to keep the rest inside.

Orin ducked into a squat as the harpy's claws grazed him. A timid brush against the canvas.

It swooped right by, then launched itself higher in the air.

Flapped its impressive wings, billowing dust Dennis's way, coating his face and infiltrating his nose.

Orin was getting it worse, with the harpy but a few feet away.

It screeched and swept in for a second attack.

Orin couldn't draw his weapon without releasing the railing. And if he did, he'd spill right down to the mattress below.

Harpies were the same as zombies. If Orin got grazed, Team Hoke would lose a lot of points.

Probably enough that they'd have to do perfectly on every other phase to win the game, or even keep up.

If he fell, then Orin was out of the game, and Dennis might as well be.

He tilted his head sideways, until it brushed his upper arm.

He wondered what Orin was trying to see. If there was

something the game was showing his son that Dennis couldn't spy from down here.

He couldn't wait a second longer. Orin was trapped, and it was his father's duty to help him.

Dennis raised his gun and took aim at the harpy.

Then with trembling hands, he fired.

Dennis missed, the shots leaving streaks in the air going above the harpy's head.

But it startled the beast, and she flew away, screeching as she dove through the air in retreat.

Orin stood straight, quickly wobbled his way to the center of the bridge and their treasure.

The air filled with more of the harpy's bloodcurdling song, then dove again at Orin.

"Pick on someone your own size!" Dennis yelled, willing to sacrifice himself if it meant saving his son.

He heard someone approaching from behind.

They'd have company any minute, and Dennis would have to choose between shooting the harpy, or eliminating the newcomers.

If he opted for the harpy, the intruders could take him out of the game, and leave his son a sitting duck. But if he chose the newcomers, the harpy would probably send Orin off of the bridge and down to the ground, if he managed to avoid the creature's claws.

His hands shook, waiting for the harpy to respond. But it avoided Dennis.

He shot and missed, then fired again, the shot flying by the harpy but nearly hitting Orin.

At least the harpy was distracted.

Orin reached for the treasure, flinching back again as the harpy swooped toward him.

Crap.

The newcomers were now in sight.

Someone hiding behind a tree, peeking halfway out from some brush, shooting.

They should have died right there, but *BOOM! BOOM! BOOM! BOOM!*

Four shots from somewhere nearby, and another pair of skeletons joined the party.

Again, they were saved.

Dennis turned toward what had to be the hidden player's general direction, half-expecting to catch a shot and turn into a skeleton himself.

He caught his breath, waiting to see what would happen.

When nothing did, he rushed over to the spot where he had heard the noise, and witnessed the rustling brush.

But by the time he got there, the shooter was gone.

Dennis looked back over at Orin as his display beeped with an alert, telling him what his eyes already were: Orin had secured the treasure, leaving Dennis to wonder what it might be.

He checked the display, and sure enough Team Hoke had officially entered phase three.

He ran back to the rope bridge, just in time to see Orin climbing down the tree on the opposite side, looking triumphant.

"Nice shooting!" Orin yelled at Dennis, pointing to the two skeletons descending the hill.

And Dennis felt a flush of something, shame or guilt, maybe budding humiliation. He was wincing inside. He'd almost shot his son, and now he had to say out loud what he was loath to admit.

"It wasn't me." Dennis pointed to where he thought the shooter was hiding. "It was someone else, over there, I think. But they were gone by the time I got there."

Orin shrugged. "It doesn't matter. We're on to phase three, with only two teams ahead of us. We can catch up."

Dennis checked his display. Sure enough, the Wilders were apparently still thriving.

And that wasn't the only thing bothering him.

Why hadn't the mystery shooter taken him out of the game when they had the chance, and it would have been so easy to do?

Simple as pulling the trigger.

"Wait. Someone might be waiting to ambush."

Orin shook his head, as if his father were being ridiculous. "It's fine, let's go."

The kid was doing an awful lot of shrugging. Wasn't he taking this seriously?

It was hard to argue with his results so far, but he sure seemed nonchalant.

Or maybe he was worried, and the training had taught him to keep his emotions inside. Like Goliath, or their instructor at the shooting range. Neither of those guys would let it show on their faces or in their body language, even if they were worried about an ambush in waiting.

Maybe Dennis was looking at this all wrong, thinking about where Orin might be taking an unintentional left when he was so obviously getting things right.

His son was tougher than he used to be when this competition started, and was naturally better at burying his outward emotions than he ever was before.

It was a hell of a game face, but if Orin expected for his opponents to never see him sweat, then he probably had to stay stoic in front of his father as well. It was a mindset, not something he could turn on and off. Like an athlete in the zone, putting the whole team on their back.

His worry turned into comfort, and again Dennis felt warm.

Proud that Orin was becoming the kind of man he needed to be in this world, and that it was his father who had nurtured his growth, by pushing him to try harder.

Dennis had no doubt, standing there at the very edge of phase three, he was a better father than his old man ever was, or could ever have been.

Chapter Twenty-One

IT WAS GETTING DARKER FAST.

Where had the day gone?

They arrived at the tournament amid the morning crowds. A boisterous cacophony that would've been overwhelming if the famili organizers hadn't been so excellent at their jobs.

The teams were divided, and through either luck or providence, the Hokes and the Wilders were placed in the same run. Though really, that made sense. Despite the fake accounts Dennis used to spy on the Wilders, he'd also stalked from his own account plenty.

And judging by Tom's actions over the years, always wanting to show off in front of Dennis, he was probably a bit jealous — or perhaps intimidated by — Dennis, and would likely have looked him up on the app as well.

To keep the game interesting, the app would have naturally paired those players most familiar with each other.

It must have been late afternoon by the time they were

dealing with the zombie sheriff and grabbing their treasure.

And the hours had flown by since then.

Dusk now teased the horizon, and an even steeper climb up to the lake. Despite their months of conditioning, and all the horse candy, his body was still throbbing. Dennis wanted to stop and rest, call it quits for five minutes at a time.

But he could never request it, being the only one on his team with a problem.

Orin kept steamrolling forward.

Dennis needed his son to admire him, and admitting what a hard time he was having would accomplish the opposite. And besides, he was still stinging from the memory of nearly turning his son into an unwitting skeleton and sending him out of the game.

"How are you doing back there?" Orin asked.

Back there?

Dennis was only a few feet behind him, giving his son space if anything. "I'm doing great."

The sun was gone, but the world was still beautiful. A nearly full moon filtered through the trees, casting shadows in an elegant pirouette across the many swaying branches.

"I think we should turn on our lights," Orin suggested.

Dennis was glad. He didn't want to be the one to suggest that they flip on their chest lamps, but he did wonder why they hadn't already. Especially as the number of unsettling sounds had increased. Some were animal, others had to be human, and there were many — Dennis was sure, though he didn't want to ask Orin — that had to be there as part of the tournament, maybe more zombies designed to keep their adrenaline pumping. The sound-track to this part of the adventure was sinister in parts, spooky in all the rest.

Squeaks and screeches. An occasional shriek amid the constant rattling. A wicked wind slicing through the trees like an army of whispers. The occasional owl was haunting them, but Dennis was always grateful when its hooting cut into the chorus, being a noise he could identify.

Orin turned on his lantern, like the headlamps used for camping, but set into his body suit, and brightened their world with a few hundred watts.

Dennis did the same and felt instantly more relaxed.

The light helped to settle his nerves, but the noises somehow seemed even louder. The crunching of their footsteps as they ascended the hill swelled into what was almost an echo.

Dennis found himself trying to walk even softer, as though terrified that something out there might hear his footsteps and come to end him, expel Dennis from the tournament that was about to change his life, and ruin the chances of his being the father he had always wanted to be.

Maybe his earbuds were amplifying every sound, and it was mostly in his imagination. Except it wasn't just the crunching of his footsteps. That damn whispering wouldn't stop, and even seemed to be getting louder.

He still wanted to ask Orin if he heard anything, but not enough to waver his faith. But sometimes he could almost make out a word, and Dennis was dying to decipher the rest of what he couldn't hear.

He found himself straining to listen harder, working to determine what those whispers might be saying.

And finally, he heard hints of what might be actual words and phrases, tickling his ears along with the rest of his senses.

It's coming.

Look out, I'm serious.

It's too late ...

Dennis had no idea if he was really hearing any of that, or if it was his percolating subconscious. The mind had a way of playing tricks, and it sounded like his might have a bagful.

He told himself to ignore it. He was only creeped out if he allowed himself to be, so that simply meant paying no mind to the whispers, and holding his focus on Orin still trudging a few feet ahead.

Run!

But that last whisper sounded like it was right over his shoulder.

Dennis yelped, spun around, and saw nothing.

The shadows kept getting darker. Light from his chest lamp was dimming, a semi-circle of illumination shrinking back like a scolded child.

The whispering intensified, same for the rustling in the forest around them.

Dennis wondered if he was going to shit himself. It was possible, with his bowels as nervous as the rest of him.

A hand grabbed him, jerking Dennis out of reach as a long black arm emerged from a nearby tree trunk, its clawed hand closing on air.

And, humiliating as it was, Dennis yelped again.

The arm reached out a second time, this time followed by something made of shadows. Twisted and vaguely, grotesquely female.

The creature yawned — or at least it opened its mouth much wider than any human jaw could manage. A lamprey-like maw, lined with several rows of razor-sharp teeth, tiers of overlapping like a battalion of teenagers crowding its way into a concert.

Orin tapped his right temple, then shoved his father forward with one hand, yelling "RUN!" as he drew his .45, pulled the trigger thrice, and sent an unholy trinity of bullets into the demon's chest.

The creature evaporated in a cloud of rainbow-colored mist, colors muted as they were swallowed by the dark.

Then the mist hardened, and the creature began to reform itself, emitting a high-pitched cackle as it did.

Dennis ran up the hill, his heart pounding, legs burning, gasping for breath, somehow managing to not kill himself even as he ran smack into a tree branch.

He heard Orin behind him, right on his tail, even though he could probably have run faster, his pistol discharging with another whine every few seconds.

The high-pitched cackle rented through the air again, echoing along with their footsteps.

Dennis didn't dare to look behind him, but he could assemble the picture well enough based on the sounds. Orin kept ending the creature, but apparently the demon-dryad was unwilling to die. It probably couldn't be killed.

That was the challenge in this part of the tournament. They had to keep running, as though they had to escape Hell itself, because the demon could never leave the borders of perdition behind.

They were nearly to the top. Dennis could hear Orin's heavy exhaling, and while his son still held the steady breath of a person in charge, Dennis sounded like someone sawing a log. Wheezing hard, his head a pounding or two from explosion.

Still, he forced himself to keep putting one foot in front of the other, refusing to fail his son.

He could see the top of the hill.

And then the river bank looming ahead in a crooked shimmering line, gleaming wet in the darkness, moonlight shining like diamonds on the waves.

Orin tripped behind him, grunting as he went down in a crunch of decaying leaves and snapping branches.

Dennis whirled around, firing wildly. But despite his bottomless bullets, he hit nothing.

At least now he could see the danger, so there must be something he could do.

The demon spread its wings at it hovered above Orin, opening its mouth even wider than before, surely about to breathe fire.

Orin groped for his gun, buried somewhere in the leaves. But he couldn't find it, and for the first time in the game, he appeared almost frantic.

This was it, Orin was seconds from becoming a skeleton, and the fury of his loss was all over his face.

This was Dennis's chance to save the day.

He simply had to do it.

Draw his gun, aim, and fire away.

But he wasn't fast enough. The demon flapped its wings for what felt like the final time, screeching as it prepared to swoop and attack, breathe fire or worse, when shots rang out from somewhere behind him.

The demon burst into another rainbow of mist, already reforming as Orin scrambled to his feet and ran over toward Dennis.

But he was already taking off, racing away the second he saw that Orin was safe, knowing his son would catch up in seconds.

And he did, grabbing Dennis by the arm and whirling him around, then dragging him toward the lake without a word of explanation.

Once there, he pointed to a line of boats docked by the shore. Small two-person canoes.

The demon was already back to cackling, and Orin

wasted no time, pushing their boat into the water, then wading in and climbing inside.

Dennis caught up and Orin extended a hand, pulling his soaking father up and into the boat.

Orin was already rowing.

Dennis gripped the side, crouched in the back, gasping for breath and unable to speak a word, staring at the demon-dryad in the distance, dissipating into a cloud of mist, then slowly reforming itself as they glided away through the water toward the opposite shore.

Good thing the demon disappeared, now that Dennis was ready to shoot it.

And with that thought came a cruel and wicked certainty.

He trembled, praying it wasn't true. Patting himself down to validate the impossible.

He couldn't have blown it that badly.

But he had, and all of his empty pockets proved it. Same for his vacant holster and hands.

Dennis had dropped his gun in the water.

At least Orin didn't know what he'd done. Yet.

Still stoic, rowing as though he couldn't get tired, his rhythm metronomic, back and forth, pushing them like God Himself blowing a sailboat across the sea.

And Dennis wasn't even helping.

"I can do that," he offered, pointing to the oars.

"I've got it," Orin said.

Back and forth and swish; back and forth and swish; back and forth and swish.

They were nearly there, the small island at the center of the lake.

Dennis wheezed, feeling miserable, like a complete and total failure.

As a team leader, as a father, and as a human being.

As least there was this last phase.

His final shot at redemption.

But if they lost, Dennis didn't know how he would ever look his son in the eye again.

Chapter Twenty-Two

APPROACHING THE ISLAND, Dennis spied a pair of skeletons sitting dolefully ashore, woebegone in the face of Team Wilder, already heading for the towering stone temple before them.

The pyramid was beautiful. Fashioned from crumbling stones and trillions of pixels. Ancient yet state of the art. Artifact and imagination.

The tower loomed at the top of a small hill.

He liked looking at the backs of Team Wilder, knowing victory was close.

Of course it came down to the four of them. Dennis would have liked to eliminate their biggest competition earlier, but this was the way fate had always intended it to go down.

Thomas Wilder had been a thorn in his side forever. He acted like he knew better, just because he had better. And that had always been bullshit. Dennis was sick of it, and today he declared no more. Never again. He would rip the crown off of Thomas's head and stomp on it.

It would help if he had his gun. Dennis would give anything to get it back.

The adrenaline rush was gone along with his weapon. Inches from victory yet miles away.

He didn't need his weapon. Guns were necessary for every player unlucky enough to be teamed without a kid of Orin's caliber. He wouldn't miss, so Dennis had it easy. If he could maneuver them both to Team Wilder, then his son could finish the job.

A little luck, a lot of determination, and a gunslinger's level eyes had gotten them this far, thanks mostly to Orin, and some guidance from Dad. The same combination would take them to the finish line.

Orin hopped out of the boat, crouching, already creeping across the shore toward the temple. He didn't have to play it lazy on his father's account.

"Wait!" Dennis called out, still in the boat but scrambling out. "I can run. Let's hurry up and catch them."

Orin turned his head. "What?"

"If we get close enough without them noticing, we can ambush them — they'll never see us coming."

"If we go much faster, we'll lose the element of surprise."

"I can be quiet."

Orin looked like he swallowed a sneer. His nose twitched and he licked his lips, like his tongue was caught flinching. "They'll hear you coming from a mile away."

That wasn't fair. Dennis knew how to be quiet. Still, no use arguing.

"Okay, then let me be the sacrificial lamb. You find a place to hide, and I'll make a racket to distract them."

"What if we called a truce?" Orin suggested. "Take a look at your readout."

Dennis did, and confirmed what he already knew.

"Exactly. We're the only two teams left. Why would we call a truce? It's us or them."

"If we're the only two teams right now, then we could collect the artifact together, and tie for first. Everyone wins."

Dennis stared at his son like the boy had lost his mind. Or he had been hit on his head and had it stolen, like credits from his pocket. "Are you kidding?"

"Why not? We've all trained hard. Mr. Wilder and Ryan both helped us out. We all deserve to win. Both families, all four of us."

"*That's* what this is all about?"

Dennis was incensed, his pores leaking lava.

"Don't you realize that you're doing exactly what they wanted you to? They were only nice to you so they could take advantage of you just like this, because they knew you'd bitch out when it came time to face off. You're giving them exactly what they want!"

"No, I'm not. I'm getting exactly what *I* want. For everyone to win. We proved we could do this, to ourselves. That's what matters. Tying for first is just as good as winning."

"You've gotta be kidding me." Orin had gone totally nuts. "Tying is not the same as winning. And I'm not sharing our prize money with Thomas Wilder, when he already has everything in life he could ever possibly want. That's like letting him win twice. It's not fair."

Orin sighed and tapped at his temple.

Then it hit Dennis like a slap on the ear.

Church bells behind his eyes, clanging at midnight.

He wanted to fall with the realization, land on his knees in disbelief.

But it was true, that wasn't a nervous tic. It was a

signal. Every time Orin had done that, some mysterious person had come to their rescue.

And now it was clear who that had been. It was obvious; he should've seen it so much sooner.

Team Wilder.

"Don't signal them." Dennis grabbed Orin by the wrist. "Team Wilder only helped us get this far to make sure that they'd face us alone at the temple. They wanted you to feel obligated, to guarantee their win. *This is a trap.*"

Cold laughter from behind him, followed by the sound of Wilder's voice. "Don't be an idiot, Dennis. We haven't been helping you. We're in to win it."

"Then why don't you shoot me in the back, Tom?"

"Because it's important to me … I want to see your face when I beat you. Turn around."

Instead of turning, he looked at Orin. "Shoot him. Let him take me out. You can still win."

"That's not going to happen. Your son isn't an idiot. He knows Ryan will shoot him the second he flinches."

Footsteps, like clomping hooves in the quiet, considering their closed circuit and current of nerves. Then Ryan entered his peripheral vision.

But … his gun wasn't pointed at Orin.

It was aimed at Tom Wilder.

One Wilder turned on another.

"What the hell?" Tom stared at his son.

"I told you I was sick of this. And that I didn't want to compete in this stupid contest. Or do any of the other bullshit you always make me do."

"Don't be ridiculous," Wilder said, daring to sound impatient. "Shoot Orin so we can—"

Ryan pulled the trigger, and turned his father into a skeleton.

Dennis whirled around, desperate to see the evidence.

Tom tried to shoot him, but his facade was a strobing charade of failure and flickering bones.

As a team leader, as a father, and as a human being.

There was a dot of red on his chest, Tom aiming at him, but it couldn't hurt Dennis any more than a fly could bite off his nose. The skeleton flickered and Dennis wanted to laugh.

But he held it inside, looking smug instead to turn down his nose at the enemy.

Wilder threw down his gun in disgust. "If you think you're going to get away with humiliating me, you're—"

Tom stopped talking.

He stared at Ryan, his eyes wide and inquiring. "What are you doing?"

Ryan grinned like a maniac, gun at the side of his temple. Same place Orin had been tapping all day.

"You can't—"

But Ryan pulled the trigger and turned into a strobing echo of his father.

"— do that," Wilder finished.

Dennis watched with an open mouth as a glowing light appeared in the center of the stone temple and Orin strode towards it.

The place lit up like the Las Vegas Strip.

Music pounded from speakers.

Fireworks exploded above them.

Heavy metal guitars wailed in the air.

Dennis wondered how silent the world would be if he removed his goggles. Probably like a forest at midnight.

The symphony of victory settled, lulling just low enough for Mr. Jones and his campfire voice to make the announcement that everyone had been waiting for.

"And the victory goes to Team Hoke!"

Dennis was lucky, to have such an industrious genius

for a son. All this time he had naively believed that Tom and Ryan were playing him, when in reality Orin had been pitting the pair against each other.

Dennis had never been so proud, not of Orin, nor of his hard work as a father.

Chapter Twenty-Three

DENNIS OPENED HIS EYES, squinted into the thin rays of sun bleeding through the barely open blinds, then tried and failed to remember last night.

It took him a minute, then it started to come. Hazy at first, then quickly rolling downhill.

Jessa was in bed beside him — @hawtestmom, until Team Hoke nabbed first place, and she officially introduced herself all over his body.

His head felt like someone had filled a pillowcase with a pile of rocks, then swung it like a bat at the back of his skull. Someone the size of Goliath.

Jessa had a long line of drool, dribbling past her chin and onto her naked chest. Sagging breasts, lacking the buoyancy and allure of what she managed to package them into, between her pushup bra and swagger. A lot like her face, now missing the makeup, and without the benefit of all those touched-up photos. He'd had a few days to get used to her.

Impossibly, he was getting bored. They did all the things she had messaged about, a few times each. He'd never had sex like that before. Jessa said the same thing, but taking into account how she bounced up and down, and side to side, with a practiced, performative, and confident ease, Dennis had his doubts.

She kept going on and on about their upcoming trip to Mexico. But his excitement had dimmed, and Dennis was wondering if he would even survive it.

But Dennis was loyal, and Jessa was a good time, so long as he kept her drinking.

Not that he should be doing it himself. And he would stop, probably the second he got back north of the border. But that trip wasn't going anywhere, and there was no way he was doing it sober. Not after he'd already started drinking, and he had to do that so things wouldn't feel so goddamned weird with Jessa. He'd never needed an icebreaker more in his life.

It wouldn't be a problem. He wasn't even going to tell anyone, because he could already imagine the reactions. Everyone at the clinic, Susan, of course. Worst of all, Orin. He'd see this situation as the failure it wasn't. No need for concern or reprehension. He would put all of the bottles back on the shelf, or dump them in the trash, exactly like he already had once before.

But first, Dennis deserved to celebrate. It was the end of an era and he'd earned it.

Orin would never want to do it again. He made that clear already. He could claim this year's title of Millennial Knight for the rest of his life, but he emphatically stated that it was out of his system forever. He was looking forward to some new challenges in his life.

He was glad to get the money. Weirdly, almost insistently so. He wanted his share transferred into his account immediately. Every credit.

"You promised, Dad," Orin had said, practically

tapping his foot, as though his father would ever try to cheat him.

He waited until the transfer went through, then probably felt sorry for being so edgy about it all, because he left Dennis alone to party with his new girlfriend, saying he'd go home with his mom, since she was still with the spectators back at Meadow Crest, waiting for the celebration to start.

He and @hawtestmom started drinking at the jubilee, then left the party to hit it harder somewhere else. Or at least more lavishly. Why celebrate in a crowd when Dennis could commemorate the occasion with @hawtestmom?

So he did, after the steak and lobster and bottle service.

Dennis was disappointed that Orin didn't want to stick around with him, and as the evening wore on, images kept flashing back. That look on his face. Like Orin was relieved that his dad was off to do his own thing.

Fine with him. It was easy to forget about when he was having the best sex he'd had in ages.

Jessa groaned and sat up. The third such morning in the last five days.

"Morning," she said with a crooked smile, wiping the drool away from her chin.

Her face withered inward, like she was trying to throttle her sneeze. Her throat made a hiccup. Something jolted her tongue, enough to push her lips out for three stuttering seconds before she could no longer hold it back.

Jessa lurched forward, then rolled over and threw up all over a pile of his clothes on the floor.

She stayed doubled over and heaving for a few moments, then she gathered her bearings, sat up straight, drool and speckles of vomit all over her sagging and slightly wrinkled breasts.

Jessa laughed like it was no big deal, just another moment doing the drool of shame.

"Sorry about that."

"No problem," Dennis said, even though it was very much a problem, and what the fuck had he been thinking? Jessa had the soul of every barfly he'd ever gone home with. Why did he ever imagine that it would be different, just because she had an ex and a minivan?

"You wanna get some breakfast?" Another laugh, too loud for this early, this hungover, or this ever. "Maybe Mexican. To celebrate."

Her smile was hopeful.

The moment was yawning, and Dennis still didn't answer. He didn't know a polite way to say what he was thinking.

He opened his mouth and—

A knock on the door.

"I've gotta get that," Dennis said, rolling out of bed, stepping right on the vomit, then shaking it off of his foot as he ran to the closet.

He threw on some clothes, not looking or caring if they matched.

"Should I hide in here?"

"Goddammit. I don't know. Give me a second to think."

If it was Susan, dropping Orin off, she would smell the sex, and the booze.

He'd promised he wasn't drinking, and he hadn't been. Until now.

He was a grown man and they weren't married, so Dennis could do what he wanted, but what would Orin say about finding another woman in his apartment?

"Just stay here," he told her. "I'll be back."

Orin would understand. Maybe even help him think of

a way to get Jessa out of there, without hurting her feelings, or ever having to talk to her again.

Susan was on her third round of knocking by the time Dennis opened the door.

But it wasn't her.

He looked past Orin, over the third-story guardrail, and down to the parking lot below. An AUTOnomous X, with Ryan behind the wheel.

"What happened? Where's your stuff?"

"I'm not staying over."

Of course. Susan was pissed. And now she wasn't going to let him come over at all.

"I understand if your mom is mad, but you're old enough to decide where to live. I already used some of the prize money to hire a lawyer, we'll fight—"

"No."

"No, what?"

"I'm using my half to get legally emancipated. I'm not staying with you or with mom anymore. She's too demanding and you … you're too selfish. I did what you wanted. Now, I'm out."

Selfish? This couldn't be happening.

Dennis was a good father; why was he being abandoned?

"You're my son, you can't just opt out of that."

"The United States legal system says differently."

"But what are you — where are you going to live?"

"I put first and last on an apartment. Ryan and I are starting a game company together."

Orin had ripped out his heart.

Dennis felt hollow, and like he was about to fall over. He wobbled in the threshold, grabbing the frame to steady himself.

He had never felt so betrayed.

"But … what about us? You can't quit on Team Hoke."

"It was never Team Hoke, it was always Team Dad.

"That's not true, son. I did it for you. So we could have a better relationship. I was trying to connect with you.

Orin shook his head. "You spent all your time connecting with your fans. It was never about me."

"I took steroids for you! So you could be a winner."

"I never wanted to be a winner. I wanted to be loved."

Dennis couldn't stand the way Orin was looking at him, his face placid. A natural, neutral expression to hide the scheming little shit that he was. That fucking hair on top of his head in a bun, like some idiot, adolescent yogi.

A wave of rage engulfed him.

He wanted to smother his son in the fire.

"I gave you everything, you little shit, you fucking pussy! And this is the thanks I get?"

Orin kept looking at him calmly, saying nothing, while his father loomed over him, heaving and drooling, rage making rivers of veins on his face.

Orin looked around the apartment, at the bottles and boxes, at all the signs of a bacchanal, then deeply inhaled, pulling the reek of his father's delusion into his nose.

"Enjoy your life, Dad."

Then he walked away.

And as he left, Dennis saw life through the eyes of his father.

What to read next

If you loved reading *Vicarious Joe* and want more Avery Blake in your life and on your kindle, you're in luck! You can start reading Analog Heart today:

Get Analog Heart Today

A Quick Favor...

If you enjoyed this book, please take a moment to write a short review on your favorite online bookstore so other readers can enjoy it, too.

Thanks so much!
Avery

About the Author

Avery Blake doesn't want you to know where she lives, or what she does. She travels the world, moving from place to place quickly to ensure she can't be tracked. It's safer that way.

When she's not looking over her shoulder, you can find her in the corner of a cafe, facing the exit, typing as fast as she can.

Also By Avery Blake